### *We were best enemies . . .*

All night long, she lay there in her bed, sobbing about how much weight she had gained off those two lousy shakes. I would have said something to her, really, but I was busy lying there thinking about how fat *I* was getting. And the more I thought about it, the more anxious I got, and the more anxious I got, the more I wanted to rush out and binge. That made me hate myself even more. I was so busy hating myself, I didn't even have time to hate Lauren. Besides, from the sound of her sobs, she was doing a pretty good job of it all on her own.

I was almost asleep when Lauren spoke for the first time in hours. "Zibby?" she asked in a whisper. "Are you scared?"

"Of what?"

Lauren sniffled. "I don't know," she said. "Never mind."

I lay there for a while, listening to her softly cry, before I answered. "I'm scared of everything, Lauren," I said.

Look for these other dramatic
titles from
**HarperPaperbacks**

*Good-Bye, Best Friend*

*My Sister, My Sorrow*

*Please Don't Go*

*Life Without Alice*

*Losing David*

# Please Don't Go

**Elizabeth Benning**

# HarperPaperbacks

*A Division of* **HarperCollins***Publishers*

Special edition printing: July 1994

HarperPaperbacks   *A Division of* HarperCollins*Publishers*
10 East 53rd Street, New York, N.Y. 10022

Produced by Daniel Weiss Associates, Inc., 33 West 17th
Street, New York, New York 10011.

First HarperPaperbacks printing: May, 1993
Originally published by Dell Publishing in September 1992, as
*Dying to Eat* by Katherine Applegate.

Printed in the United States of America

HarperPaperbacks and colophon are trademarks of
HarperCollins*Publishers*

10 9 8 7 6 5 4 3 2

*For Michael*

Special thanks to Karen Schwartz-Phaup, R.N., C., M.H.S.A., Program Coordinator, Eating Disorders Program of Tucker Pavilion at Chippenham Medical Center in Richmond, Virginia, for her assistance, patience, and insight.

This diary belongs to

ZIBBY LLOYD

Room 4-B

**PRIVATE!! KEEP OUT!! THIS MEANS YOU!!**

Go snoop in someone else's diary, okay?

# November 8

## FOOD INTAKE

### BREAKFAST

1 8-oz. glass skim milk
1 bowl shredded wheat with skim milk
1 orange
1 multivitamin

### A.M. SNACK
Carrot sticks and apple slices

### LUNCH
1 high-protein milk shake
½ cup broccoli and cauliflower medley

### P.M. SNACK
1 1-oz. slice low-fat cheese
1 slice whole-wheat bread

Dinner
    One each: Snickers bar, Almond Joy, Butterfinger, and Reese's Peanut Butter Cup. One entire chocolate cheesecake. One box Ding Dongs. One pint rocky road ice cream. One pint mint-chocolate-chip ice cream. One pint double-dark-chocolate ice cream. And for dessert: one large bag of Hershey's Kisses.

Okay, so maybe I lied about dinner.

The truth is, I had broiled flounder. With lima beans, no less.

But a girl can dream, can't she? And let's face it, this bogus food diary doesn't exactly make for juicy reading.

Other thirteen-year-olds write in their diaries about guys, or parties, or school. Or maybe even their secret fantasies.

I write about broiled flounder.

Correct me if I'm wrong here, but I seem to be missing something.

Like a life.

Oops. I'm doing it again. Negative thinking. Whenever I do that, Dr. Patterson says I'm supposed to take a deep, cleansing breath and think about something positive. And not something positive like warm chocolate-chip cookies, either. Dr. Patterson's my psychiatrist here. She's very big on cleansing breaths. As far as I'm concerned, air is air,

4

but who am I to argue? She's the one who went to shrink school.

This journal is Dr. Patterson's idea, too. Keeping track of what I eat is supposed to help me change my attitude toward food. But when I write *cauliflower*, I think *chocolate*. I don't exactly see how that's helping my attitude problem.

I'm also supposed to be baring my soul in this diary. You know, putting my feelings down on paper, in between the skim milk and the tuna fish and the endless parade of good-for-you vegetables. Dr. P. says writing down my emotions will help me feel better about myself.

Fine, Dr. Patterson. Here's what I'm feeling. I HATE IT HERE I HATE IT HERE I HATE IT HERE.

I've been here at Hopeless House two whole days and it's very clear to me that a terrible mistake has been made. I do not belong here. There are sick people in this place. Very sick people. I am not sick. I am hungry.

When I say "Hopeless House" in front of Dr. P., she just shakes her head. "It's called *Hope* House for a very good reason, Zibby," she said during my therapy session this morning. "A lot of the kids staying here are very sick. Some will be chronically ill for their whole lives. A few may even die. You're lucky because you can get better, if you let us help you."

"But I don't need to be here," I argued. "There

5

are kids here with leukemia. And diabetes. And AIDS. What I have is like a pimple compared to their problems."

"Bulimia can be a life-threatening disease," Dr. P. told me in that get-with-the-program voice she uses. "You have a very serious eating disorder."

Yeah, right. A cold can be life-threatening, too, if you stand out in the rain in your underwear. But I've got things under control. Really. And deep breaths and diaries are not going to change the way I live my life.

I'll tell you what would change my life. A couple of pounds of chocolate and a one-way ticket out of this place.

SOMEONE, GET ME OUT OF HERE!

Sorry, Dr. P. I have now written down my feelings, and I do not—repeat, DO NOT—feel better about myself. So much for your diary theory.

She told me I could be in here weeks. A couple months, even. I told her no way.

I've escaped from some pretty tough places. Pep rallies. Family reunions. Orthodontist appointments. Even after-school detention.

Mark my words. I'm busting out of here, too.

Gotta go now. Here come the Calorie Cops. (Otherwise known as nurses.) It's time for our evening snack.

It's a pretty safe bet they won't be serving Snickers bars.

# November 10

Dr. P. wants me to write in this thing as often as I can. "Write what?" I asked her. "Pretend you're talking to a friend," she said. "A friend who'll never judge you. One you can always trust."

I groaned. "I've never had one of those."

"So fake it," she said with a smile.

That's how Dr. P. is. Nothing you say surprises her. She's youngish, with wild black hair she ties back with scarves, and glasses that constantly slip off her nose. I guess you'd say she's pretty, but she could afford to take off a pound or two. (That's something I always notice about a person right away—their weight.) She told me she used to be a bulimic herself when she was younger. It took her years to get better, because there weren't any programs around like the one at Hopeless. I was lucky, she told me.

Dream on, doc.

So anyway, here I am again, thanks to Dr. P. They make you sit in your room for half an hour every evening and write or meditate. If you can't think of anything to write about, they give you a topic. Like, for example, "What I Ate on My Summer Vacation."

Tonight I've picked my own topic—"Why This Place Makes After-School Detention Look Like a Wild Party." I mean, talk about uptight! They monitor your every move here. You can't pee without someone knowing about it. Every moment of our day is planned for us. They have group therapy (shrink time), occupational therapy (finger-painting time), and therapeutic recreation (jog and sweat time). There are special times for us to do our schoolwork, to write in our journals, to see our families. I feel like I've joined the Marines.

Most of the kids here don't have to follow these insane rules. They're here because they're not sick enough to be in a real hospital, although they do need constant medical attention. It's me and the other EDs who are in prison. (That's Eating Disordered, I discovered today.) We're at the end of the hallway on the second floor of Hopeless, kind of off by ourselves.

Most of our time is spent on eating. Or to be more accurate, on *talking* about eating. You would not believe the boring movie they forced me to sit through this morning. All about eating disorders. A real Academy Award contender. I pointed out that I wouldn't be here if I didn't already know how to be a bulimic, but they made me watch it anyway. The least they could have done was serve popcorn.

Besides, I've already read lots of books at the public library about my problem. I went there early one Saturday morning, because I knew there wasn't much chance I'd run into someone from South Somerset Middle School. I dreaded the idea that someone I knew might walk up to me and say, "Good book you're reading?"

This is what I found out. Everybody's gotta eat, right? Well, some people just don't do it as well as other people. On the one hand, there are anorexics. Basically, they starve themselves. They'll eat two raisins, and say, "Wow, am I stuffed!"

Me, I have sort of the opposite problem. I'm what they call "bulimic." That means I go on binges, where I eat pretty much everything in North America.

The binge eating is bad enough. But the worst part, the disgusting part, the part that makes me want to throw up just thinking about it (and I'm very good at throwing up), is that after bingeing comes purging. Purging means you get rid of whatever you ate.

Good luck trying to explain *that* to anybody. I made the mistake of trying this afternoon.

I'd decided to take a little tour of my new prison. The nurse on duty, Ms. McGehan (they call her Ms. McG.) told me I could go for a walk, as long as I stayed on the second floor. She made a really big deal out of it, too. Like I was Columbus, exploring the New World. "Five minutes and no more, dear heart," she warned. She's got this nice Irish accent and incredibly long white hair that she pins up with great combs. If she weren't a prison guard, she'd probably be perfectly nice.

I headed off, peeking into rooms as I went. Pretty soon I came to this little African-American boy in room 2-B. He was bald, completely. With big brown eyes the size of half dollars. Probably about seven or eight, I figured. He had an intravenous tube in his right arm. The IV was connected to a bottle of clear fluid hanging from a tall metal pole.

"Hey," he said. "Come on in. You know how to play checkers?"

"Are you kidding?" I said. "I'm practically the world champion."

He narrowed his eyes. "You got any cash?"

"You play for money?"

He reached for the checkerboard on the nightstand by his bed. "Quarter a game. Can you handle it?"

I whistled. "Pretty high stakes."

"Come on," the boy repeated.

I leaned against the door, hesitating. The truth is, sick people make me nervous. I've never really been around any until now, and I'm afraid I'll say something stupid. I can be kind of blunt sometimes.

Instead of going in, I just sat there, staring at the boy's round head glistening in the afternoon sun.

"I'm bald because of chemo," the kid said suddenly, as though he could read my mind. "Chemotherapy for cancer. It's like really strong medicine." He sounded like he'd given the speech before. "So anyway, that's why."

"Oh," I said. "Well, it works on you. You look very dashing. Like Michael Jordan."

He laughed, and after another moment, I went in and sat down in a chair next to his bed. A little part of my brain was wondering if I should be sitting so close, but I remembered from my health class last year that cancer isn't contagious.

"I'm Spencer." He handed me a stack of red checkers.

"Zibby."

"That your first name or your last name?"

It was my turn to laugh. "My real name's Elizabeth, but my little brother couldn't hack that many syllables. He made up Zibby, and it stuck."

"I like it. It works on you," he said. His wide smile revealed two missing front teeth.

Suddenly I gasped as my eyes fell on his legs. Where there should have been two lumps beneath the blanket, I saw only one and a half.

"Bone cancer," Spencer said matter-of-factly. "But I'm getting a special leg fitted soon. Dr. Gordon says it'll be my bionic leg and I'll run faster than Carl Lewis someday."

I placed my checkers down, one by one, avoiding his eyes. Spencer's words were hopeful, but something in his voice told me he was scared, deep-down. I didn't want to think about that too hard. It would just remind me that I was feeling pretty scared myself. What if I really *was* sick? As sick as Spencer, in a different way? I definitely didn't want to start thinking about that.

"So what are you in for?" Spencer asked after a while.

I looked up. "You sound like we're in prison."

Spencer giggled. "We are, in a way."

"I have bulimia," I replied. I realized with a start that I'd never actually said those words out loud before.

"Oh." Spencer nodded. "You're one of those starving people." He cocked his head and eyed me critically. "You don't *look* like you're starving."

"No, that's anorexia," I corrected. "Anorexics don't eat enough. Bulimics—" I paused. "Bulimics eat too much, and then they purge."

"What's purge mean?"

He had to ask. "Well, it means you get rid of what you ate." There. I'd avoided the gross details. Always a wise move.

Spencer fiddled with a checker. "Get rid *how*?"

What an inquiring little mind. I hate kids with

inquiring little minds. "*You* know," I said reluctantly. I was practically whispering. "You can take, um, laxatives, to help you, um—"

"Go to the bathroom?"

A bright kid, Spencer. I nodded. "Or you can—" I cleared my throat, which was sore, as usual, from all that purging. "Regurgitate."

"Say what?" Spencer demanded. "You mean you *make* yourself puke?"

I threw back my shoulders and forced a smile. "I prefer regurgitate. It's so much classier."

Spencer smiled back. "Man," he said, shaking his head. "I'd give anything *not* to throw up from the chemo. And you're throwing up on purpose!"

When he put it that way, it did seem a little odd. I don't know why, but I wanted this little kid, this perfect stranger, to understand. "See, I don't *want* to throw up," I said. "But this feeling comes over me, sort of frantic and out-of-control, and I start eating and I can't stop. While I'm eating, the world kind of disappears, and I forget everything that's bothering me. It's like I'm numb, you know?"

Spencer nodded. "Like at the dentist, when he gives you novocaine."

"Except it's my brain that's numb, instead of a tooth. But the bad part is that when I'm done eating, the numbness wears off. I start to feel so awful, and so afraid of getting fat, that I throw up, even though I don't really want to. After a while it sort of gets to be a habit." I sighed. I knew how bizarre it sounded. It was hard to explain, and even harder to understand, unless you'd been there.

"You shouldn't worry about getting fat," Spencer replied earnestly. "You're a babe."

I couldn't help laughing. I know how I look, and "babe" isn't the first word that comes to mind. The bulimia has really wrecked my appearance, which, to be honest, was not that hot to begin with. I have my mom's round green eyes and strong chin, and my dad's curly reddish-brown hair. Unfortunately, I also inherited his height. I've been the tallest girl in my class ever since preschool. My weight's more or less average, although it's a miracle, given what I eat on a binge. That's why I have to purge so often. I'm always right on the edge of fat. If I'm not careful, someday I'll look in the mirror and see the Goodyear blimp staring back.

Anyway, the bulimia hasn't helped me in the looks department. My hair is as dry as a Brillo pad, my cheeks are puffy, and my neck glands are so swollen I look like I have a serious case of mumps. Worse yet, my teeth are starting to rot from all the stomach acid when I vomit. Let's just put it this way: Christie Brinkley and Elle McPherson have nothing to worry about. I won't be appearing on the cover of *Glamour* or *Seventeen* anytime soon.

"So move, already," Spencer urged.

I shoved a checker one space.

Spencer studied the board intently. "Were you born with bulimia?" he asked.

I smiled, trying to picture a two-year-old me stuffing down Twinkies at three thousand calories a binge. "No," I said. "I mean, I've always had trouble with my weight. You name the diet—I've tried it. Grapefruit diets, rice diets, liquid shake diets. But this—my bulimia—only started the last year or so."

"They'll fix you here," Spencer said as he eased a checker forward cautiously. "They can fix anybody here."

"There you are!" Ms. McG. appeared in the doorway. A little boy stood next to her, holding her hand. "You promised just five minutes, dear. And around here, we expect you to keep to your promises."

I rolled my eyes. "The warden," I whispered.

"If you leave the game early, you still owe me a quarter."

"Watch this guy," Ms. McG. warned. "He'll take you for every penny you've got."

"Put it on my tab," I said, smiling at Spencer.

Ms. McG. led the little boy over to the bed across from Spencer's. "That's Alex Fury," Spencer said. "My sometimes roommate. He needs a kidney transplant."

"Hey, Alex," I said.

"Ask him something about basketball," Spencer urged. "Anything."

As it happens, I know a bit about basketball myself. My dad's a real fanatic. "Who was the NBA's Most Valuable Player in 1987?" I asked.

Alex groaned. "Give me a break. Too easy! Magic Johnson, L.A. Lakers."

I nodded. "Not bad at all."

"Come along, dear," Ms. McG. said, touching me on the shoulder.

"See you, guys." I followed Ms. McG. into the hall. "Is Spencer going to be okay?" I asked quietly, when we were out of earshot.

"If the cancer doesn't spread," she replied. "There's hope. There's always hope, dear."

I thought about the way his covers had laid there. And about how he'd never run around like other little kids. Suddenly a wave of disgust came over me. I hated myself. Kids like Spencer were really sick, sick in ways they couldn't help. I was right when I'd told Dr. P. I don't belong here. I don't deserve to be around kids with so much courage, not when I don't have any.

I wanted to eat and eat until I passed out, just to make the guilty feelings go away. But they don't let you do that here. They want you to suffer. They're good at it, too. Really good. That much I can tell already.

# November 12

I can't think of anything to put in my diary today. Dr. P. suggested writing about how I ended up here at Hopeless. Fine. Why not? I've got to keep my pencil moving or Ms. McG. will catch on. She's a smart one. Smarter than most teachers. If things don't work out here, she could always get a job monitoring study halls at my school.

Anyway, since you asked, Dr. P., the way I see it, I wouldn't be here if Ms. Klinefelter had better hygiene. (Okay, so maybe I'm exaggerating a little.) But if she hadn't insisted on teaching an entire lesson on negative numbers with a very large booger dangling precariously from her very prominent nose, then I wouldn't have had to comment on it loudly, and she wouldn't have felt compelled to ask me to vacate class. And that's when all the trouble really started.

There I was, facing yet another detention. What choice did I have but to discreetly slip out of school and head for the 7-Eleven down the street? I needed a little fix, just a tiny carbohydrate rush. A couple dozen donuts to tide me over until lunch.

Unfortunately, I was a little short of cash—if you can call a grand total of twenty-seven cents in savings "short." Not nearly enough to cover the donuts. Let alone the box of laxatives.

Fortunately, I was wearing my extra-baggy jeans. They're the ones I wear when my weight sky-rockets (which is pretty much every other day). Not only are they very comfortable, they can easily accommodate a couple boxes of Krispy Kremes with room to spare.

The clerk was busy trying to fix the Lotto machine, so I was able to fit two boxes of crullers into my waistband without any trouble. I untucked my shirt so it nicely covered the evidence. The laxatives, it turned out, fit perfectly into my breast pocket. Sure, I looked like I was developing a little unevenly. Or like I was into cardboard lingerie. But they've seen it all at the 7-Eleven.

I picked up a newspaper to buy (it was all I could afford), acting very cool and talkative. That's part of the art of shoplifting. You don't just rush out. You saunter out. I prefer a sort of casual swagger. I've perfected it in front of the mirror. And if you can, you buy something. It always throws them off guard.

The clerk was a young guy with a wispy mustache that looked an awful lot like a dust bunny. He stared at my rectangular right breast a moment longer than was strictly necessary, but I just gave him a haughty look. Then I paid for my newspaper and headed for the door.

Unfortunately, that was right around the time my Krispy Kremes decided to head for the floor.

They plopped out the bottom of my jeans with a surprisingly loud thud. (Stale, probably.) But I'm one cool customer. I kept right on walking, like I was wearing the latest in fall footwear.

"Hold it," the clerk ordered.

I reached for the door. My heart was beating like a drummer in a heavy-metal band. But I managed to smile my best "who, me?" smile.

"What are those?" he asked, peering over the counter.

My eyes dropped to the floor. "Reeboks," I replied.

"No." He shook his head, pointing to the three inches of box protruding past the hem of my jeans.

"Oh, *those*," I said. "How did those get there, I wonder?"

I considered making a run for it. But running down the street trailing cruller crumbs seemed so uncool, somehow. And besides, there was the little matter of the cop who'd just pulled into the parking lot on his break.

So one thing led to another. The cops called my parents. After the 7-Eleven manager agreed not to press charges because I was a minor, my

19

parents called my school counselor and arranged a meeting. At first, I thought I was going to get off easy. But the last straw came during the meeting with my counselor, Ms. Binkley, when she noticed the calluses on my middle finger and my index finger. I'd gotten them from sticking my finger down my throat to make myself throw up. After a while, your fingers get rubbed raw from scraping on your upper teeth. Ms. Binkley put together all the evidence—my calluses, my swollen glands, the laxatives and donuts—and voilà! One bulimic.

"How long have you been bingeing and purging, Zibby?" she asked.

"What are you talking about?" my mom interrupted nervously. "Zibby doesn't—"

"Zibby does," I admitted. I knew the game was up. I was scared to death to talk about everything out loud. But to tell you the truth, it was a huge relief, in a way, to get caught. I was sick of pretending, and sick of myself.

I don't think my parents were exactly surprised, in their hearts. There had been plenty of clues, if they'd bothered to see them. They'd just sent me to our family doctor last month because of my glands, for example. He'd said I probably had a virus. Dr. Shaw's a nice guy, but he's about one hundred and ten and not exactly playing with a full deck, if you know what I mean.

But there'd been other things, too. The way food disappeared overnight. The money I kept borrowing for school projects (actually binges). The way I'd go to the bathroom right after dinner and stay there forever with the water running, so they couldn't hear me throwing up.

You'd think my parents would have been prepared. I've always been the troublemaker in the family. Don't get me wrong. I don't go out and rob little old ladies or anything. I just mouth off a little in class now and then. But compared to Cheryl, my sister, who's a senior, or Brad, my brother, who's in fourth grade, I never quite seem to measure up to my parents' high standards.

My guess is, my mom and dad didn't really want to know the truth. After all, they're both busy attorneys. They have a perfect house and a perfect dog and three perfect children. Who wants to think the kid in the middle is some kind of food freak?

I have to say, though, that they took the news about my problem pretty well. There was a lot of crying and stuff (mostly on the part of my mom, who's a champion weeper). But when the tears were over, they told me they loved me and that we'd get through this problem together.

After the big revelation, Ms. Binkley contacted the Eating Disorders Clinic right here in Somerset, Indiana. She made an appointment for me to see

Dr. Patterson that very afternoon. I met with Dr. P., she admitted me to Hopeless, and the rest, as they say, is history.

To think I owe it all to a booger. I don't think I'll ever forgive Ms. Klinefelter.

# November 13

I'm convinced I was adopted. Somewhere out there is my real family. They're miserable and fat and eat Krispy Kremes for breakfast, lunch, and dinner.

My parents deny this, of course, but then, my parents deny everything. They deny, for example, that they favor Cheryl and Brad, even though it's true. My mom thinks Cheryl is perfect. My dad thinks Brad is perfect. No one thinks I'm perfect, unless you count Floyd, our guinea pig. He thinks anyone's perfect, as long as they'll feed him.

I tried to explain all this in family therapy today. Not that I exactly *wanted* to or anything, but Dr. P. gets kind of annoyed if you just sit there staring at the hole in the knee of your jeans without saying a word. She seems to think we're all supposed to talk or something. You might as well ask Floyd to chat. Talking's not something my family's had a lot of practice at. Oh sure, we open our mouths and sounds come out. But I have a feeling that's not what Dr. P. means when she asks us to communicate with each other.

Cheryl tried to get the ball rolling, of course, because she wants Dr. P. to like her. It's very important for Cheryl to be liked. I guess that's a good quality to have when you're a cheerleader. Cheryl's been a cheerleader for as long as I can remember. When she grows up, she wants to be a cheerleader adviser. Either that, or president of the United States. Cheryl's very ambitious.

So anyway, Cheryl was the first one to speak up today. "I think Zibby needs to work on her attitude," she told Dr. P.

"What attitude?" I snapped.

"*That* attitude," Cheryl explained calmly. "You're so . . . well, *negative* all the time, Zibby. It's all in how you look at things. You always see the glass half-empty, instead of half-full."

That's Cheryl. The human Hallmark card.

"How about that, Zibby?" Dr. P. prodded.

"It's easy for *her* to say," I said. "Cheryl's thin and beautiful and everyone adores her because she's so darn *perky* all the time."

"What's wrong with being perky?" my mom demanded. She reached for Cheryl's hand and gave it a little squeeze. I forgot to mention that my mom is a *former* cheerleader. Perkiness is also very important to her. Me, I have never been accused of perkiness, which I believe proves my adoption theory once and for all.

"This is exactly what I've been telling you, Dr.

P.," I said, shooting an angry look at my mom. "Cheryl can do no wrong. Brad can do no wrong. But *everything* I do is wrong."

"I can *so* do wrong," Brad declared. "I'm not some goody-goody—"

"*I* know that, phlegm-brain." I rolled my eyes. "The point is, Dad thinks you're a perfect little angel." I turned back to Dr. P. "Trust me, he's not."

"Zibby, hon," my mom said in her best I'm-an-attorney voice, "your dad and I realize that Cheryl and Brad aren't perfect—"

Cheryl made a little pouty face.

"But it just seems like you go out of your way to be troublesome. The, um—" she cleared her throat, "shoplifting thing, for example. Or take something even simpler, like your weight—"

"The doctors say I'm a perfectly normal weight for my height!" I exploded.

"Zibby's right," Dr. P. interjected calmly.

"But if she'd just watch the snacks—"

"Mom, it's not *my* fault I got Dad's genes!" I cried.

My father looked out the window. He does a lot of that during therapy, but he hardly ever talks. Mostly he just looks sort of queasy.

"Genetics does play a role in determining weight," Dr. P. agreed. "Have you ever considered that maybe you've been sending Zibby confusing messages about the importance of her looks?"

Finally. Somebody on *my* side! For a moment, I felt really grateful to Dr. P. Then I remembered that it was her fault I was even *having* this stupid argument with my family.

"I want Zibby to understand that looks can be important to her self-esteem," my mom argued.

"But the self-esteem has to come first," Dr. P. replied. "First, she has to learn to like herself."

"Excuse me," I interrupted. "Am I invisible or something? Would you please stop talking about me like I'm not even here?"

It was all downhill after that. By the end of the session, everybody was mad at everybody else. My mom was crying, Cheryl was glaring, Brad was sulking, and my dad— well, my dad was looking out the window.

Later, Dr. P. told me she thought my family was really beginning to make progress. If you ask me, she's the one who needs to have her head examined.

She sees a full glass. I definitely see an empty one.

# November 14

"Choose five words that best describe you."

That was today's assignment in group therapy. In group, the three of us EDs living at Hopeless get together in this big recreation room with a bunch of outpatient anorexics and bulimics. (Outpatients live at home but come here for therapy on a regular basis.) There are maybe ten of us all together. The youngest is ten, the oldest looks like she could be my mom's age.

I sit with the other two Hopeless girls, but I wouldn't exactly call us buddies. There's Rachel, a fifteen-year-old anorexic who's been here forever and acts like she owns the place. They've been sort of mainstreaming her lately, which means that she often gets to live with roommates that are sick in the normal way. And she doesn't get the watchdog treatment that other EDs do. She's going to be discharged soon, I think, and start seeing Dr. P. as an outpatient. Good riddance, is my feeling. The girl's a real pain. She's the kind of person who'll give you lots of free advice on how to run your life, whether you asked for it or not.

Apparently, Rachel's such a success story that this time around they stuck her with Kendra, a new girl, figuring Rachel would be a big inspiration. Let's just say I have my doubts. Rachel really lords this over Kendra, even though Kendra's a year older than Rachel. Kendra's what they call "bulimarexic." That means she binges and purges like me, and in between binges she starves herself, like Rachel. Kendra follows Rachel around like a puppy. It's really pathetic. I may just have to give her some of my patented Zibby Lloyd Assertiveness Training.

Of course, it's hard to be assertive when you weigh next to nothing. Kendra's so skinny I swear you can see every bone in her body. Rachel says she used to look like that, too, but she's put on weight since she got here. I pray every night I don't gain any more weight before I find a way to get out of this place.

That was the weird thing about the lists we made in group today. When we compared them, every girl in the room had described herself as "fat." Even the anorexics, who, trust me, are not exactly porkers. A lot of us used the word "bad," too, especially the bulimics.

"It's interesting how so many people in the group used the same words to describe themselves," Dr. P. said, "whether they were anorexic or bulimic.

I heard a lot of negative words, words that said *I don't like myself very much*." She looked around the room. "I'll let you in on a little secret about all those negative words. Nobody's sure exactly what causes eating disorders, or why some people become bulimics and other people become anorexics. But we do know that people with eating disorders are always trying to make bad feelings disappear. They don't think they can control whether or not they feel bad. But eating—that's one thing they *can* control."

I yawned. More psychobabble, as I liked to call it. Dr. P. has all these crazy theories about us EDs. That's why I especially hate group therapy. They expect us to all feel the same way, and I'm an original.

"When I was a bulimic," Dr. P. continued, "I felt better when I was bingeing. For a little while at least, nothing else mattered but food."

I gazed down at my hands. Sure, I'd said the same things. So what?

"The problem was, I couldn't seem to make the good feelings I had while I was bingeing last. And after I purged, well—" she shook her head, "then I *really* felt lousy."

I stole a glance at her. For a split second I felt this weird sort of hopefulness. Was it possible Dr. P. actually understood what I'd been feeling?

Nope. Nobody else on earth did, I reminded

myself. Why should she? I'm alone. Strictly solo. My problems are my own business, which is fine by me. That's what I'm used to, after all.

"Anorexics tell me the same thing," Dr. P. added. "Starving themselves makes them feel better. It gives them power over their lives." She smiled. "But starving won't make the bad feelings inside go away. And neither will bingeing."

While Dr. P. continued her talk, some of the girls, like Kendra, got very emotional. After a while, all that bawling really started to get on my nerves.

"Why are you crying?" I demanded, turning to Kendra.

"Because I never knew so many people felt the way I do," she said between sobs.

"Zibby, I'd like to hear what you're feeling right now," Andrea Shepherd suggested. She's a social worker who helps Dr. P. out with group therapy. Andrea's always full of energy and enthusiasm. She's also very big on hugging people. I guess we all have our faults.

"Zibby?" Andrea repeated. "Would you like to share with us?"

I hate it when they start talking about sharing. It's like joining the Girl Scouts or something. Everybody's so *sincere*.

But they were all staring at me, so I had to say *something*. "I'm feeling like I could really go for a couple gallons of pralines and cream ice cream," I answered. "With hot fudge sauce."

A few people laughed, but most of the girls looked at me like I'd just burped in church.

"I know what you mean," a redhead named Cynthia piped up. She's a junior at a high school in a town about fifty miles from Somerset. I guess this is the closest ED group she could find. "I used to think about food every waking moment—that is, when I wasn't eating it, or throwing it up," Cynthia continued. "But I've been in therapy for eighteen months now, and I haven't binged and purged in a long time. That doesn't mean I still don't have my bad days. But if you give it a chance, you'll get better, too, Zibby."

"I don't want to get better," I said. It was the truth. Maybe I *had* been kind of miserable bingeing. But I'm a whole lot *more* miserable here at Hopeless, not bingeing.

Cynthia reached over and patted my arm. I discreetly curled my lip, and she backed off. "Just remember, we know what you're going through, Zibby," she said. "We're all friends here."

Wrong. No one knows what I'm going through. And I don't have any friends. I haven't had any in quite a long time. Not since I discovered what a reliable friend food can be. When I'm bingeing, nothing else matters. All my troubles disappear. What friend can claim to do that?

31

Anyway, it's time to go. Evening snacks. A couple pathetic graham crackers. Besides, I've been rambling in this diary long enough. You know, I hate to admit it, but I'm kind of getting used to writing in this thing. It beats talking to Rachel and Kendra. And I can say whatever I want without anyone talking back. Dr. P. was right. It *is* a little like having a friend. A very quiet friend.

Of course, it's no substitute for chocolate, but even so . . .

# November 15

You know, the one thing this place had going for it was the fact that I had my own room. It's not a bad room, either. I've got a big comfy bed, and there's a huge window overlooking the flower garden in the backyard. It's not exactly the Hilton, but it'll do.

But this evening I walked in after a study session, and there was this girl lying in the bed across from mine. I couldn't get a good look at her, because a doctor and two nurses were hovering over her and the curtain was pulled around her bed. I did glimpse an IV pole, though, like the one Spencer had for chemo.

"Who's that?" I asked Ms. McG.

She herded me toward my bed. "You have a roommate."

"But this is my room," I insisted.

"You're going to have to share," she replied. "Besides, it'll do you good to have some company, dear. Who knows? Maybe you'll get to be good friends."

"Don't bet on it," I grumbled.

The doctor pulled back the curtain a few inches.

The name on his pocket reads "Dr. Rhodes," but everybody calls him "Dr. Steve." I recognized him because he's kind of hard to miss, what with being absolutely gorgeous. He has these intense, dark eyes, and beautiful dark skin the color of milky coffee. He looked up from the chart he was holding and smiled at me. "Hey, there, Zibby," he said.

I felt my cheeks burn. I hate it when I blush around guys. "How long will she be here?" I asked, pointing to the other bed.

"That's hard to say."

"Can you give me a rough guess?"

He laughed. "Sorry."

Then I thought of something. "How come she's in here with me? Aren't you a heart doctor?"

He sat down next to me on my bed. Up close, he looked even more like a soap opera star, just like everybody said.

"Your roommate had a very close call this morning," Dr. Steve explained quietly. "She's an anorexic, and her blood pressure got so low that she passed out on the stairs at school. The bump on her head wasn't bad, but we're monitoring her heart to make sure the rhythm stabilizes. When your potassium level is too low, it can cause dangerous heart irregularities."

I shifted uncomfortably. "Of course, that can't happen to people with, um . . . my problem, right?"

"Yes, I'm afraid it can, Zibby. Bingeing and purging can seriously upset your body chemistry."

I decided to change the subject. "So what's that bottle by her bed for?"

"NG feedings," Dr. Steve said. "Nasogastric. We insert a thin tube through the nose, down the esophagus, and into the stomach."

What a disgusting thought. "Through your *nose?*" I repeated.

"It's the best way to get nutrition into a patient who's in crisis like this. The liquid has glucose, fat, protein, vitamins, minerals—the works."

"I'd rather go to McDonald's."

Dr. Steve laughed. "We only use NG feedings in extreme cases. If you keep working hard to get better, you'll never have to worry about that." He stood. "Now, no loud parties in here for a while, okay? She's going to need some rest."

I groaned. As though Rachel and Kendra were real party animals.

After Dr. Steve and the nurses left, I tiptoed over to the white curtain separating the beds. Carefully, I peeked around it. My eyes followed the IV tube down to the girl's nose. The sight was so awful I had to close my eyes for a minute. Then I opened them again, because I realized what I'd just seen.

I knew this girl. Worse yet, I didn't like this girl.

Lauren Kent. I'd known her since we were little kids, and she'd been getting on my nerves ever since. See, Lauren had always had this one teensy little character flaw. She was perfect. We're talking perfect with a capital P here, folks.

I stared at her in disbelief. Lauren Kent, Little Ms. Perfect, was an anorexic? Who would've guessed it? True, she was incredibly thin, but lots of girls are thin. And you never really gave it much thought because Lauren always wore really bulky clothes. Oversized sweaters, baggy pants, that kind of thing. Besides, she was so busy being perfect, who cared if she was a little on the thin side? Or even a *lot* on the thin side?

Now, I'm really a very nice person. Ask anybody. I get along with just about anyone, even people I have a perfect right not to get along with. Like my orthodontist.

Or Mr. Seavers, the vice-principal, who's honored me with more detentions than anyone in the history of South Somerset Middle School. (With the possible exception of Jack McAllister, who got shipped off to reform school last month.)

But Lauren Kent? She made it so tough to like her.

Start with her looks. She'd always been gorgeous. Even in kindergarten she stole people's boyfriends. Including mine. Harry Possessorski, to be precise, who'd declared his undying love by sharing half his box of Goobers with me. One coy little smile from Lauren and it was all over. She was the kind of little girl who always wore prissy dresses and shiny black patent leather shoes. How can you trust a five-year-old who refuses to wear sneakers?

Of course, as she got older, Lauren just got prettier. Straight, glossy blond hair, past her waist. Huge blue eyes with lashes that you'd swear were fakes. Not an ounce of fat on her.

Not that I was jealous, mind you. I had nice hair, too, if you like it brown and frizzy. And I had nice eyes. Just not quite so many lashes. And as for fat—well, I had an ounce or two. Or three. But there was just more of me to love. And it's not like I was ever overweight. I just wasn't pencil-thin.

And then there were her grades. Lauren didn't just get A's, she got straight A-pluses. She got A-pluses from teachers who, in their entire twenty-year teaching careers, had never given an A-plus. She got A-pluses in everything. If they'd graded recess, she'd have aced that, too.

Of course, I *could* have gotten A-pluses, if I'd cared to. I was always in the 99th percentile on standardized tests. I just didn't apply myself. I was an underachiever. You might even say I overachieved at underachieving.

Still, because of all my untapped potential or whatever, I got stuck in a lot of accelerated classes with Lauren as we were growing up. Sometimes we even sat next to each other because of our last names—you know, Kent and Lloyd. This was unfortunate, because Lauren was one of those people who just *loved* school. Whereas I was one of those people who just loved hating school. Some teachers even called me disruptive, but I was misunderstood. I just tried to liven things up when they got dull.

Like that time at the beginning of sixth grade. We were suffering through a lecture on pronoun use. Lauren was sitting in front of me in a state of rapture. She just couldn't get enough of grammatical errors. Well, it was still pretty warm out, and the windows were open so there was a fly or two buzzing around. When one landed on my desk, I very politely asked Lauren if I could borrow just one little piece of her hair. I thought she nodded yes, so I yanked one out and used it to lasso my fly. It was really cool when he flew around, like having an airplane on a leash. But Lauren, snitch that she was, had to make a big deal out of my borrowing a little hair. Like she didn't have plenty to spare. I had to stay after school and write an essay on cruelty to animals.

But it wasn't just the fly incident. Lauren and I ended up competing over everything.

We took ballet together. She was thin and graceful. I was thick and klutzy. She got to play the

Sugarplum Fairy in *The Nutcracker Suite*. I got to play a tree.

Later, we took gymnastics together. She was thinner and even more graceful. I weighed more than everyone except the coach. She got a gold medal in the balance beam at the state championships. I got a sprained ankle when I slipped on a sweaty gym mat.

It was always like that. Is it any wonder I didn't like Lauren? Not that I let on how I felt, though. We more or less ignored each other. But she was always there, making my life miserable without even knowing it.

And now, here she was at Hopeless House. My very own roommate. What a comedown for her.

I guess I can admit this here, since nobody but me's ever going to read this thing. I've spent the whole day feeling like someone gave me a present I've always wanted. I know that's a lousy way to be, but hey, I never claimed to be a saint.

I can't wait for her to wake up. I hope I'm not in therapy. After all, someone's got to welcome Lauren to life here at Hopeless.

# November 16

Unfortunately, Lauren woke up while I was in group therapy this afternoon. When I got to my room, she was sitting in her bed wearing a hospital gown. Without her usual sweaters, I could see how thin she really was. Her arms looked like twigs.

A petite woman in a prim dress sat in a chair next to Lauren's bed. Lauren's mom. I recognized her from gymnastics meets. She never missed one.

"Welcome to prison," I said cordially.

Lauren stared at me out of the deep hollows of her eyes. "Zibby?" she whispered.

"Small world, huh?"

Lauren just kept staring. I think she was as stunned to see me as I'd been when I first saw her last night.

"How long have you been here, Zibby?" Ms. Kent asked in her soft voice. You always had to strain to hear her.

I hopped on my bed. "Forever," I said. "Actually, a little over a week. It just *seems* like forever."

"Why are *you* here?" Lauren asked doubtfully.

I gave a nice, casual shrug. "Scarf and barf."

Ms. Kent's hand flew to her mouth. "What—"

"Bulimia," I interrupted. I cast Lauren a knowing look. "Sort of the opposite of you. If we could just trade problems, we'd be all set."

"I do not have a problem," Lauren replied. She said it slowly, carefully, and very, very angrily.

"Lauren, honey, you know what Dr. Patterson said—"

"I was just tired, and I fainted," Lauren said. She pressed her mouth into a thin line. "End of story."

Ms. Kent fumbled with the pink hankie in her lap. She cleared her throat. "Lauren, remember your contract—"

"Mother!" Lauren snapped.

Perfect little Lauren, bawling out her own mother? Would wonders never cease?

"We all agreed," Ms. Kent continued nervously, "that if you didn't live up to the terms of your contract with Dr. Patterson, you would have to be hospitalized."

"So you were seeing Dr. P. as an outpatient?" I asked politely.

Lauren glared at me.

"Yes, she was," Ms. Kent answered. "Once a week. Lauren had signed a contract—"

"I can speak for myself!" Lauren cried.

"I know all about contracts," I said. "Everybody does them. Mine says I have to be good or I lose privileges here. As though I *have* any privileges here!"

"Good?" Ms. Kent repeated uncertainly.

"You know. Not puking."

She made a little scrunched-up disgusted face. Normally I would have felt humiliated, but Lauren seemed to be feeling humiliated enough for both of us.

"So what was your contract?" I asked Lauren.

"Lauren was supposed to gain a pound every two weeks until she reached a reasonable weight," Ms. Kent answered.

"I *am* a reasonable weight," Lauren muttered.

I almost laughed. I mean, the girl looked like a walking skeleton. But I was used to anorexics talking that way. Kendra thought she was enormous, and she was nearly as thin as Lauren.

"Hey, gorgeous."

My mom came breezing in with Cheryl right behind her. Lately, particularly after that last session with Dr. P., my parents have taken to calling me "gorgeous." It's supposed to boost my self-esteem or something.

Suddenly my mom stopped in midstride. "Jenna?" she said, staring in surprise at Ms. Kent. They knew each other from all the ballet and gymnastics and PTA meetings.

"Hello, Lynn," Ms. Kent said in a tiny, embarrassed-sounding voice.

My mom looked over at Lauren. "Hi, sweetheart," she said. "Gee, I'm sorry to see you here."

Lauren rolled over and pulled her sheet up to her chin.

"Lauren's anorexic," I piped up. "We've worked out a deal. She's going to give me all her meals, and I'm going to binge on them."

No one laughed. I should have known. Hospital humor is wasted on the healthy.

Cheryl bounced over and hopped on my bed. She bounces everywhere she goes. "I brought you all your homework, Zib."

"You expect me to thank you for that?"

"So the girls will be keeping up on their schoolwork?" Ms. Kent asked.

My mom pulled over a chair and sat next to her. "Oh, yes. There's a time set aside for studying each day, and a tutor who comes in to help the girls with their homework. Cheryl's been picking up Zibby's homework for her."

"I could pick up Lauren's too, if you like," Cheryl offered. My sister, the good citizen.

"Thank you, dear, but I think I should take care of that myself," Ms. Kent replied. She smiled at Lauren. "In any case, Lauren shouldn't have any trouble keeping up. She's a straight-A student."

Lauren pulled the sheet all the way over her head.

Cheryl patted me on the leg. "So this is great, huh? You'll have a roomie now. You guys can be friends—"

"It'll be like one big sleepover, Cheryl," I interrupted. "We'll tell ghost stories and make popcorn. Only Lauren won't eat it and I'll barf it up."

Cheryl pursed her lips. Ms. Kent chewed on a thumbnail. My mom smiled tensely. "Zibby, remember what Dr. P. said about negative thinking," she advised.

I looked over at Cheryl and started to feel bad. After all, she meant well. I knew she thought I could be cured by pep rallies alone. "Sorry, Cher," I mumbled.

"That's okay, Zib," Cheryl said brightly, instantly recovering. She's used to my mood swings. "I'm going to go pee, and then you can look over those homework assignments and see if you have any questions." She leaped off the bed. Halfway to the bathroom door, she suddenly stopped. "Oops," she said sheepishly. "I forgot."

"Forgot what?" Ms. Kent asked.

"They lock the bathroom," I explained. "Except for the first thing in the morning, when we get to take a shower all by our itty-bitty selves."

"They *lock* the bathroom?" Lauren demanded from beneath her sheet.

"If you want to go, you have to call a nurse. She

44

stands outside the door the whole time to make sure you're behaving."

"Mother, you have got to get me out of here!" Lauren cried.

"What could happen in the bathroom?" Ms. Kent asked.

Parents. They can be so naive. "Lots of things," I replied. "I could smuggle some food in. Or I could try to purge by taking laxatives or throwing up. We ED types are very wily, you know."

Ms. Kent looked unconvinced. "But Lauren—an anorexic—shouldn't have to be restricted that way. Maybe we should ask for a room change."

As though Lauren's problem were superior to mine. "Anorexics are just as bad," I pointed out quickly. "They'll go in there and flush down food they pretended to eat. Or they'll try to exercise like crazy."

"I see," Ms. Kent said softly. She looked as if she was about to cry.

My mom reached over and patted her hand. "It'll be okay, Jenna," she said. "The girls are in the best possible care."

"I hate it here," Lauren moaned. "It's like a prison."

"You've got that right," I replied with grim satisfaction. "Welcome to Hopeless House, Lauren."

# November 16, 11:30 P.M.

I'm not supposed to be writing in my journal this late, but then, rules were made to be broken, I always say. I'm sitting here with my bedside light covered up so the night nurse won't catch on that I'm awake after lights out. Who are they to tell me when to hit the sack, anyway? I've always been a night owl. Anyway, I'm writing again (twice in one day! a new world's record!) because of something that just happened with Lauren.

I was lying here minding my own business, when all of a sudden, just after lights out, Lauren tried to pull out her feeding tube. Ms. McG. came by just in time. Good thing, too, because I wasn't sure what to do—root Lauren on, or call for help. I sort of admired her initiative. I'm not sure I would have had the nerve.

Ms. McG. gave her a stern lecture. A few minutes later she came back with two other nurses. Ms. McG. was carrying a pair of straps that go on the sides of the bed to hold your arms in place. Lauren started crying hysterically, but Ms. McG. and the other nurses just strapped her arms down and told Lauren that if she wanted to be released, she'd have to earn their trust.

I'd never seen them do that to anybody, which made me realize that Lauren must be a serious case. I even started to feel the teensiest bit sorry for her when she was sobbing. This was very annoying, because, as I believe I've mentioned, I don't much care for Lauren. It's very difficult to dislike someone and feel sorry for them at the same time.

After the nurses left, Lauren kept bawling, so I did the only thing I could do under the circumstances. "Would you please shut up?" I asked. Very politely, of course.

"I don't belong here," Lauren moaned.

I wasn't about to argue with her. I'd heard her fight with her mom and the nurses. She didn't give up easily.

"I don't, really I don't," she repeated.

"I do," I said matter-of-factly. It was true. I knew I had a problem, a disgusting, horrible problem. I knew I couldn't control it. That didn't mean I thought Hopeless House was going to make my problem go away. Or that I wasn't going to escape at the earliest possible opportunity. It just meant I was realistic.

"All I want to do is lose a couple more pounds," Lauren said, sniffling.

I wasn't about to touch that one, either. I'd tried

arguing with Kendra about her weight. I'd lost the debate.

"Look, I'm trying to get some sleep," I said. "Could you save it for someone who's interested?"

Silence. I wondered if I'd been too rude. But you have to admit, she wasn't the ideal roommate.

"Zibby?" Lauren asked after a few minutes had passed.

"What now?"

"Could you come here for a minute?"

I lay there, debating. It was obvious that she was going to keep bugging me. I figured I might as well find out what she wanted and get it over with.

I flicked on my light and walked over to her bedside. Up close, in the semidarkness, her bony features made her look almost scary.

"Zibby, could you undo my straps?"

I put my hands on my hips. "Why?"

"They hurt. I can't sleep like this."

I looked at the straps. They were made of that sticky Velcro stuff. It would be easy for me to undo them. "What do I get out of the deal?" I asked.

Lauren smiled her ghostly smile. Her lips were cracked, and her skin was a soft shade of yellow-green. She looked like an actor in a horror movie. "You get me to shut up," she suggested sweetly.

She was putting me in a difficult position.

Whom should I side with—the authorities I didn't trust, or the girl I didn't like?

"Please, Zibby," she urged. "We're in this together."

She had a point. And what did I care? At least I could get some sleep. I undid the straps. Next to hers, my arms looked huge.

"Thank you, Zibby." Lauren rubbed her wrists.

"Now will you shut up and go to sleep?" I demanded.

"Zibby Lloyd!"

I spun around to see Dr. Steve standing in the doorway. He did not appear to be in a good mood.

He marched over and reattached the restraints. Lauren gave him an angelic smile. "I'm sorry." She said it so sweetly it gave me a sudden craving for donuts. "It was Zibby's idea."

"Oh, pul-eeze," I cried.

Dr. Steve walked me over to my bedside. "I know you were just trying to help Lauren," he whispered to me. "But you're going to have to trust that we're doing the right thing, okay?"

"I just wanted some peace and quiet," I muttered.

I should have known Lauren couldn't be trusted. The lousy snitch. Had I forgotten the fly incident in sixth grade?

Of course, I probably should have known she was an anorexic, too. It amazes me that I never caught on to her secret. I guess it's possible no one at school knew about me, either. Of course, they will now. Somerset's a small town, and my sister Cheryl has a big mouth, so it's just a matter of time. I might as well have taken out an ad in the *Somerset Times*.

But still. I never would have guessed Lauren Kent could have a zit, let alone a problem like anorexia. I suppose there were clues, if you knew what to look for. She was obsessed with dieting, for example. Lauren was always trying one diet or another so she could stay nice and skinny for gymnastics. Whenever anyone wanted to know how many calories were in something, you could always count on Lauren. She was like a walking food encyclopedia.

And she was getting awfully, awfully skinny. At first, girls were jealous. "How does she stay so thin?" everyone asked. But lately, people had started talking about how Lauren was getting *too* thin. For the most part she hid it with bulky clothes, but you know how it is in gym class. Everybody sees everybody, for better or worse. Man, do I hate gym.

I keep thinking about this time about a month or two ago when I should have caught on to Lauren's problem. Lunch was just about over, and I'd headed off to the girls' bathroom over by the gym. It's the one farthest from the cafeteria, and hardly anybody ever uses it around lunchtime. That makes it a great place to throw up in relative privacy.

When I got there, the bathroom was empty. Perfect. I'd bought a dozen or so candy bars out of the cafeteria vending machine and eaten them in the hallway when no one was looking. I was feeling pretty rotten by then, that awful cloud of guilt that comes over you after a big binge.

I went to the last stall and leaned over the toilet. By then I was pretty good at barfing on command. Sometimes I could just tense my stomach muscles and do it. But that day I was having some trouble. I had to put my fingers way down my throat for a few seconds before I could start that familiar gagging sensation.

When I was done throwing up, I wiped my mouth with some toilet paper and wiped off the seat (sometimes my aim isn't so great). I flushed the toilet and thanked goodness no one was in there to see me. I always look like death warmed over after I throw up. My face gets all sweaty and my eyes get bloodshot and sometimes the barf gets in my hair. Not, all in all, a pretty picture.

I eased open the door to the stall and my mouth dropped open in shock.

There was Lauren. She was standing over the trash can, dumping out from her monogrammed canvas purse the bag lunch her mother had obviously made for her.

She must have come in while I was throwing

up. I wondered how much she'd heard. "I think I'm getting the flu," I said quickly, by way of explanation. I walked over to the sink and rinsed off my face. As usual, I looked hideous.

"Too bad." Lauren snapped her purse shut. "I, uh—" She looked at her purse, then at me, then at her purse again.

"Your mom make meat loaf or something?" I said sympathetically, nodding at the trash can where she'd dropped her lunch.

"I have to go," Lauren said suddenly. "Honor Society meeting." She smiled faintly. "Hope you feel better."

So there we were. I was throwing up food. Lauren was throwing food away. But neither of us realized we had more in common than just our mutual dislike.

I wonder if there are lots of girls at Somerset Middle School like Lauren and me, all of us walking around with the same secret. Dr. P. says I'd be amazed at how many anorexics and bulimics there are, especially girls in middle school and high school. And the dumb thing is, none of us will admit it to anyone, so we'll never really know. We'll all keep thinking we're the only ones in the world with this problem. Pretty darn funny, don't you think?

# November 17

This morning, Lauren tried to apologize to me.

"I'm sorry I lied last night," she said sweetly. "I just panicked."

I rubbed my eyes. "I guess I should inform you that I am not a morning person. Please don't talk to me until I'm awake."

"When will that be?"

"About ten this evening."

Dr. P. appeared in our doorway. "Hello, ladies."

"Hi, Dr. P.," I replied. I found myself smiling, in spite of the fact that I hadn't quite decided how I felt about her yet. It's awfully hard not to like Dr. P. For a nosy doctor, she seems pretty nice. Still, she is *awfully* nosy.

Dr. P. glanced over a chart she was carrying. "What happened last night, Lauren?" she asked gently.

Lauren looked over at me. I could tell she was preparing to lie again, so I glared back. "I, uh . . . these things hurt my wrists," she moaned. "Can't you take them off, please? I promise I'll be good."

"I'll do better than that," Dr. P. replied. "We're going to take you off the NG feeding today, Lauren."

Lauren let out a loud sigh of relief.

"But we have rules here at Hope House, as I told you," Dr. P. continued. "If you don't follow them, you'll have to go back on the feeding tube. And if you try to remove the feeding tube, we'll have to use the restraints again. Understand?"

Lauren nodded.

"Now, I know this is tough for you, hon. But you're going to get better, if you work at it." Dr. P. looked at me and winked. "Zibby'll help you out, won't you, Zib?"

*Zibby would rather die.* "Yeah," I answered. I wondered if Dr. P. could tell I didn't mean it. Shrinks have these built-in lie detectors in their brains.

"Today you'll be getting to know everybody and seeing how the program works, Lauren," Dr. P. said. "I'll meet with you and your mom and dad later in the day, okay?"

Lauren made a face, but Dr. P. didn't react. She just smiled and patted Lauren on the shoulder. "Any questions, you just ask Zibby."

Great. Just what I needed. I felt like pointing out that when I baby-sit, I prefer to get paid by the hour.

Dr. P. left, and moments later, the nurse named

Ms. Lansky hustled in. She's a big, tall woman with short gray hair and a voice that makes you long for earplugs. Everyone calls her "Sarge."

"Morning, ladies," she said briskly. She unlocked the bathroom and held open the door. "You first, Zibby."

Lauren cast me a frightened look. "I told you," I said. "The Calorie Cops watch your every move." I jumped out of bed and walked to the bathroom. "They leave you no shred of dignity," I sniffed as I passed Sarge.

Sarge grinned. "Everyone's a critic."

I closed the bathroom door behind me and took a deep breath. These were my only real moments of privacy all day. Until I'd been admitted to Hopeless, I hadn't realized how much time I spent by myself. When you're bulimic, you do everything in secret. Now they were making secrets impossible.

When I came out, Lauren was sitting on the edge of her bed. Her tubes were gone, and so were her restraints.

"Cut you loose finally," I remarked.

Lauren didn't answer. I guess she was busy trying to remember how to walk. She was so wobbly that Sarge had to help her to the bathroom.

A few minutes later Lauren emerged, pale and hunched over. Probably stomach pains. Rachel told me anorexics get them a lot. Sarge led her back to bed and pulled the sheets over her. "Cold?" she asked.

Lauren nodded. Sarge found an extra sweater in Lauren's dresser and helped her put it on. "Back in fifteen minutes for weigh-in," Sarge said. "No funny business, now."

Lauren sat there in her bed, staring straight ahead as she rubbed her stomach.

"Cramps?" I asked, just to be polite.

Lauren nodded.

"Maybe you're getting your period."

"I got it a while ago, but then it stopped. I haven't had it in a long time." She leaned toward me. "What did she mean about weigh-ins?" she whispered. There was a look of terror in her blue eyes.

I shrugged. "They weigh everybody three times a week. Every morning, same time, no exceptions."

Lauren bit her lip. "Dr. Patterson said they won't let me out of here until I hit my target weight." Suddenly her eyes lit up. "Zibby?"

"What now?"

"Can we wear whatever we want when they weigh us?"

"Are you kidding?" What an amateur. "They make you wear these stupid hospital gowns with the peekaboo backs. And trust me. They know all the tricks in the book. That's what Sarge meant by funny business."

"But I can wear socks, can't I? I'm so cold."

I'd noticed that most of the anorexics in group therapy were always whining about how cold they were. Sometimes, after a long period of bingeing, I was the same way. I guess it had something to do with all the changes in your body. "Sure, you can wear socks," I answered.

"Could you do me a favor, Zibby?"

"Why not? It worked out so well last time."

Lauren shrugged. "I said I was sorry."

"So what do you want?"

"Could you get me some socks out of my drawer? I'm still sort of wobbly."

I sighed. If this girl thought I was going to turn into her personal maid, she had another thing coming. Still, she did look awfully cold. Her lips were even a little blue. I walked over to her chest of drawers with a loud sigh.

"Top drawer, I think," Lauren instructed. "Grab them all, okay?"

"All of them?"

Lauren nodded.

I removed six pairs of socks and dropped them on her bed. "Great," she said, glancing at the door. "Could you hand me my purse, too?"

I pulled it off the dresser. "I'll bet you have servants at home, don't you?"

Lauren laughed. "Hurry," she urged.

I gave her the purse. She fished in her wallet

and pulled out a big handful of change.

"If you're planning on bribing the nurses, don't bother. I already tried."

Lauren poured half of the change into a sock. Then she threw off her covers and pulled the heavy sock onto her foot. I watched in disbelief as she did the same thing with the other foot. "Very tricky," I said with admiration. "But you'll jangle when you walk."

Lauren smiled slyly. "Not if I wear the rest of these pairs." She pulled on the remaining socks and wiggled her toes. "Not bad," she said. "This'll raise my weight for sure."

"I have to admit, it's ingenious," I agreed. "Especially on such short notice."

Just then Sarge returned. "Ready, Zibby?" she asked.

"Ready as I'll ever be."

I put on my robe and followed Sarge down the corridor to the little room they used for weigh-ins. The big scale loomed before me. I hesitated. I knew my weight had gone up some more. My stomach was so big I looked as if I'd swallowed a basketball. They told me it was because of all the laxatives I'd been taking before I got to the hospital. It would take a while for my body to get back to normal, and in the meantime, I'd be retaining a lot of water. Well, it may have been water, but as far as the scale was concerned, it was *pounds*.

I handed Sarge my robe, took a deep breath, and closed my eyes as I stepped on the scale. "How bad?" I asked, opening one eye.

"Half a pound more," Sarge informed me as she jotted it down on my chart.

I felt my heart sink. "I am such a pig," I cried.

Sarge put her arm around me. "This is absolutely normal, Zibby," she said. "I told you about the water weight. It'll pass. You're a perfectly normal weight for your height." She helped me off the scale and we headed down the hall. "The important thing is to think about the inside you, not the outside you," Sarge advised.

Bad advice, since the inside me was obviously getting fat. Tears were forming in my eyes, but I didn't want Sarge to see them. It would just get her started on a long heart-to-heart talk about my "obsession" with weight. And I despised those.

I walked in high gear back to our room. When we got there, Sarge helped Lauren out of bed. She didn't seem to notice Lauren's multiple socks. "I feel awfully weak," Lauren protested. "Maybe I should wait until tomorrow."

"Off you go," Sarge said.

"Don't waste your time arguing, Lauren," I said. "Sarge never takes no for an answer."

While Lauren was gone, Rachel and Kendra stopped by. "Where's the new girl?" Rachel asked. "We wanted to say hi."

"With the Calorie Cops."

"I already got weighed," Kendra said in her thin wisp of a voice. "I've gained two whole pounds in the last week." She patted her stomach. "I look like a blimp."

Just then, Lauren returned, frowning. Sarge followed her in, carrying Lauren's socks.

"The old sock trick," Rachel said. "I tried that one once, didn't I, Sarge?"

Sarge helped Lauren into bed and pulled the covers over her legs. "As I recall, you tried drinking a couple of gallons of water right before weigh-in, too."

"Give it up," Rachel advised Lauren. "She knows tricks you haven't even thought of yet."

"Comfortable, Lauren?" Sarge asked.

Lauren crossed her arms over her chest and didn't answer.

"Call me if you need anything." Sarge turned to leave. "You girls make Lauren feel at home, now."

Rachel stepped closer to Lauren's bed. As usual, she was wearing lots of makeup. Her hair was expertly curled and cemented with hair spray. Rachel is attached to her curling iron like other kids here are attached to IVs.

Rachel smiled brightly. "I'm Rachel, and this is Kendra," she said. "We're on the ED ward too."

"Just one big happy family," I offered.

Rachel ignored me. Like Cheryl, she thinks I have an attitude problem.

"Kendra goes to J.F. Kennedy Middle School, and I go to private school in California." Rachel loved to tell people that. "How about you?"

Lauren didn't answer.

"She goes to South Somerset," I volunteered. Rachel looked disappointed. "We can't all be snobs like you, Rach."

"I'm recovering from anorexia," Rachel continued, "and Kendra's recovering from bulimarexia."

"I'm recovering from Rachel," I chimed in. "She'll really get on your nerves if you're not careful."

Rachel rolled her eyes. "Anyway, Lauren, I'm going to be going home soon."

Lauren perked up when she heard that. "How'd you manage that?" she demanded. "Tell me."

Rachel hopped onto her bed. "Well, you have to do what the doctors say, and reach your target weight—"

"Forget it."

"That's what I said, too," Rachel replied. "But after a while, you start to realize that you're not in control."

"I am *so* in control," Lauren snapped. "How else would I have been able to lose so much weight? I just need to lose a few more pounds, and then—"

"The thing is, your obsession with your weight is

controlling you," Rachel said. "Really. I've been there."

"Nobody knows how I feel."

"I do," Kendra said softly.

"No, you don't. No one does."

"You'll have to forgive Rachel," I told Lauren. "She's a true believer. She's been here so long she thinks she's part of the staff."

"Shut up, Zibby," Rachel snapped. "Just because you don't want to get better doesn't mean Lauren doesn't."

"I'm fine just the way I am, thank you very much," Lauren said.

"See?" I said. "She's hopeless, just like me. We like it that way. Pretty soon, Lauren and I are going to bust out of this joint, right, Lauren?"

Lauren looked surprised, but then she nodded. "Right."

"Lauren, I see you're making new friends already."

It was Ms. Kent. She was carrying a bag full of extra clothes.

"We'd better get going," Rachel said. "We'll see you later at group, Lauren."

I felt victorious seeing them leave. But what had I won? Lauren? I didn't even want her on my side.

Ms. Kent took out a blue flannel nightgown and handed it to Lauren. "Here, honey," she said.

"Let me get you out of that awful hospital gown."

Lauren sat there passively while Ms. Kent helped her undress. It seemed pretty weird, if you asked me. I mean, the girl was thirteen, for gosh sake, and she was letting her mom undress her?

When Lauren stood to slip on the nightie, I looked away to give her some privacy. But before I turned my head, I noticed something strange—a layer of light-colored hair on Lauren's back. Come to think of it, she'd had it on her arms, too. Kendra had told me about that in group. Lanugo, it's called. Your body starts to grow extra hair to compensate for all the heat you lose from being so thin.

I stared at Lauren as she climbed back into bed. She was growing hair in some places, and losing it in others. One spot on her head was nearly bald. Her long thick hair, the hair I'd always envied, was thin and dull.

A wave of nausea came over me. What were we doing to our bodies? We looked horrible, both of us. The only difference was that I at least knew it. Lauren wouldn't even admit it to herself.

Maybe we really were hopeless. Still, there was something kind of satisfying about having someone to be hopeless with.

Even if I didn't exactly like her.

# November 18

I gotta admit, Lauren's not the sweet little thing I thought she was. Mealtime with her turned out to be very entertaining. She may be thin, but she can put up quite a fight.

Dr. P. said Lauren could eat in our room for a few days, until she felt stronger. She even suggested that I eat with Lauren, to keep her company. I started to protest, but the truth is, I didn't exactly like eating with Rachel and Kendra, so I kept my mouth shut. Usually we go down to the dining room, which is hard for us EDs, because we all have our special eating rituals. You can't binge or refuse to eat when you've got an audience of nurses and other kids staring you down.

At lunchtime, Sarge showed up with our meal trays and explained the rules to Lauren. "You get half an hour to eat on your own," she said as she removed the top of the tray and set it up in front of Lauren. "After that, if you still haven't finished your food, one of the nurses will sit with you for another half hour while you eat."

Lauren looked over at me, her eyes filled with terror.

I shrugged. "Why do you think I call them Calorie Cops?"

Lauren stared at her food. There were a few chunks of broiled chicken, half of a small plain baked potato, some carrot sticks, and some banana slices. Not exactly my idea of a binge. "I can't eat all this!" she protested. "No way. I'll balloon overnight. This is ten times the amount of food I'd eat in a day!"

"Ms. Brady selects your food very carefully," Sarge said patiently. "She keeps the portions very small at first, so you won't feel overwhelmed."

"Do you know how many calories are in a medium banana?" Lauren demanded. "One hundred and five calories!" She looked at me for support. "One hundred and five! You expect me to *eat* that?"

"I'll eat it for you," I volunteered, smiling at Sarge. I just said it to annoy her. Bananas aren't exactly on my hit parade of binge foods.

"That'll be enough out of you, Zibby," Sarge warned, shaking a finger at me. "Although I must say your generosity is touching."

"I'm a very generous person," I agreed. "I'll eat anyone's food."

Sarge turned her attention back to Lauren. "The nutritionist gave you bananas for two reasons.

They're high in potassium, which is very important for your metabolism. And bananas were one of the few fruits you didn't mark on your trigger-food list this morning."

All the EDs had to fill out a "trigger food" form for Ms. Brady, the cook. We marked all the foods on the list that we thought were "scary." Anorexics listed foods they were afraid would make them fat. Rachel, for example, has this horrible fear of anything with sugar in it. Last week she ate a cookie for the first time in a year. As for me, I marked all the foods that I knew would start me bingeing. Chocolate, of course, was at the top of the list. But snack foods, like potato chips or donuts, came in a close second. Ms. Brady looks at our lists when she prepares our meals. At first she leaves our trigger foods off altogether. Then, little by little, she starts adding them in.

"I wanted to mark bananas on my list," Lauren said. "I wanted to mark everything. But Zibby said you'd grade me down if I checked off all the food on the list."

Sarge cast me an annoyed look. "Zibby is not always a reliable source of information. You're not competing for grades here, sweetie. You're not competing for anything."

I shrugged and took a taste of my chicken pot pie. It was not one of Ms. Brady's better efforts. "I only mentioned grades because I thought it would work for Lauren," I explained innocently. "She's very academically motivated."

Sarge narrowed her eyes. "Thank you, Dr. Lloyd."

"What happens if I don't eat?" Lauren asked. She poked at a banana slice with her fork.

"I'm glad you asked," Sarge responded. "If you refuse to eat, even after sitting with the nurse, then we add up all the calories you didn't eat, and we serve you a special concoction that tastes a little like a vanilla shake. You have to drink enough to compensate for the food you didn't eat."

"Rachel says they taste like ground-up chalk," I offered helpfully.

"Then we give you a half hour to drink up the shake."

"And if I don't—"

"If you don't drink that," Sarge continued, "you lose out on all your privileges. No recreation therapy, no group, no TV, no nothing."

"Some privileges," Lauren said with a dry laugh.

"She makes a good point," I said to Sarge.

"Your pot pie is getting cold," Sarge responded.

Lauren shook her head. "Well, I can tell you right now I'm not going to eat."

"I want you to try not to focus on the food itself so much," Sarge said gently. "We're going to be teaching you new ways to eat, Lauren. You'll have even more control over your diet. But you'll be healthy, too."

"I *know* how to eat," Lauren growled.

"The first thing I want you to do as you taste your food is to count mouthfuls. Don't just chew it up once and spit it out for the flavor."

Lauren looked surprised.

"Oh, we know all about the ways you like to eat. But there are better ways. I want you to try to chew each bite of food at least five times. Do you think you can try that today?"

"I am not eating this crud."

"You think this is bad, wait'll you see the meat loaf on Thursdays," I said. "Personally, I don't believe it's really meat. It's some kind of space-age petroleum product—"

"Thank you for your critique, Zibby," Sarge said, but I could tell she didn't really mean it. She handed Lauren a piece of graph paper. "This is for you, Lauren. We want you to understand that you're responsible for any changes you make here. You're going to be graphing your weight on it."

"Not in this lifetime."

I almost spit out my pot pie. Who'd have guessed Lauren was such a wise guy? I had thought "Gee whiz" was about as snappy as her comebacks got.

Sarge stayed completely cool, just as I knew she would. That was the annoying thing about the Hopeless staff. No matter how hard you tried, you couldn't get a rise out of them.

"Enjoy your meal, hon," Sarge said to Lauren. "And if you're feeling afraid, please call me. The most important thing you can do is talk to us about your feelings. Then they won't seem so scary." She glanced over at me. "Or talk to Zibby. I have a feeling you two have a lot in common."

Yeah, like our mutual dislike.

I ate in silence for a few minutes, fantasizing about Milky Way bars. I took this to be a sign of improvement, since yesterday I'd fantasized about Snickers bars. At least I was leaving out the nuts in my daydreams.

After a while, Lauren picked up her knife. I wondered if she was going to eat, after all. But no. She was just cutting her food. Cutting it into the teensiest little pieces you can imagine. She worked at it for about ten minutes. You would have needed a microscope to see those chicken particles by the time she was done.

"I hate these people," Lauren muttered. "What makes them think they know the first thing about food?"

"Wait till the Nutri-nag hour," I warned her.

"Nutri-nag?"

"They make us take this nutrition class. It's worse than health class at school. Major-league boring."

"When do we get to exercise?" Lauren asked. "I can't wait to do some jogging."

I almost laughed. The girl could barely walk, and she was all excited about jogging? "You won't get to do any exercise if you don't eat," I explained. "That's what Sarge meant about taking away your recreation therapy privilege."

"But I *have* to," Lauren insisted. "If I don't, I swear I'll go crazy."

"Even if they do let you exercise, they have all kinds of rules. Like they'll maybe let you do twenty sit-ups at the most. Or have five minutes on the exercise bike."

Lauren didn't answer. She was staring intently at her pulverized food. I watched as she picked up the two little pats of margarine on her tray. She checked the door. Then she carefully deposited the margarine underneath her mattress.

"Not bad," I said, nodding. "But it won't work as a long-term solution. They're bound to find out. These people are like detectives."

"You won't tell, will you?" Lauren asked. She sounded a little nervous.

"No," I answered. "It's kind of entertaining."

"Hey, Zibby!" Spencer rolled into our room in his battery-powered wheelchair. "Long time no see. You owe me money, by the way."

"I'm good for it," I said, laughing. "Spencer, meet Lauren."

"Hey," he said.

Lauren didn't answer. She was spooning her

potato into a potted plant on her nightstand.

"Why's she doing that?" Spencer whispered.

"It's a new method of plant feeding."

"Has she got the same problem as you?"

"Not exactly. Lauren's not what you'd call a big eater."

"Hey, what was your name? Spencer?" Lauren said suddenly. "Come here."

Spencer gave me a quizzical look and rolled over to Lauren's bedside.

"You like chicken?" Lauren asked.

"I like everything."

"Here." Lauren handed Spencer her plate. "Enjoy."

Spencer examined the minuscule chicken bits. "This isn't chicken," he said. He made a face and returned the plate to her. "This is some kind of dog food, right?"

"It's chicken, trust me. Please eat it," Lauren pleaded in a low voice.

"No way."

"I'll pay you."

Now Spencer was interested. "Ten bucks," he said.

"Five."

"Seven fifty."

There was a wild, desperate look in Lauren's eyes. "I haven't got it on me, but I'll get it from my mom tonight, okay?"

Spencer looked doubtful. "Well, okay," he agreed at last. "I won't eat it, but I will get rid of it for you."

"Hurry," Lauren urged. "The nurse'll be coming back any second." She shoveled the plate of food into her napkin. But when she lifted the napkin, it split in two, sending slop all over her tray.

"Oh gosh, now what?" she asked frantically. There were actually tears in her eyes. For a moment I felt sorry for her. She had the same panicky look I got in the middle of a binge.

"I know," I said. "Put it in one of your socks."

"Perfect!" Lauren exclaimed.

"I'm going to be transferred down to this end of the hall," Spencer said, laughing. "You guys have more fun at lunch."

Lauren filled a white sweat sock with the chicken goop.

"I'm not wearing that thing," Spencer warned.

"Here," Lauren said frantically. "Catch."

She tossed the goop to him, but unfortunately, her aim was a little off. The mush-filled sock hit Sarge square in the face, just as she stepped into the room. It exploded like a water balloon. Chicken slop went everywhere.

I tried, really I did, but I couldn't stop myself from laughing. Neither could Spencer. I laughed so hard I had to get Sarge to unlock the bathroom before I wet my pants.

Sarge took it pretty well, too. "I always have loved Ms. Brady's chicken," she commented as she wiped her face with a tissue.

I'm not sure Lauren heard. She was cowering under her sheets, sobbing. I don't think she's completely got the hang of questioning authority yet.

She never did eat anything. Sarge got her a fresh tray and sat with her. When Lauren still refused to eat, Sarge brought her the shake with all the minerals and vitamins in it. Lauren wouldn't drink that, either, so she wasn't allowed to leave our room all day. She went through the same thing at dinner. She gave up on the food sock concept, but she cut up her food in the same strange way, and she tried to hide a roll under her pillow. This time Ms. McG. caught on to that, too.

By that night, Lauren had two whole shakes to drink and she was still putting up a fight. But when Dr. P. came by and pointed out that the next step was going to be the feeding tubes again, Lauren gave up. She drank both shakes down without a word. All night long, she lay there in her bed, sobbing about how much weight she had gained off those two lousy shakes. I would have said something to her, really, but I was busy lying there thinking about how fat *I* was getting. And the more I thought about it, the more anxious I got, and the more anxious I got, the more I wanted to rush out and binge. That made me hate myself even more. I was so busy hating myself, I didn't even have time to hate Lauren. Besides, from the sound of her sobs, she was doing a pretty good job of it all on her own.

I was almost asleep when Lauren spoke for the first time in hours. "Zibby?" she asked in a whisper. "Are you scared?"

"Of what?"

Lauren sniffled. "I don't know," she said. "Never mind."

I lay there for a while, listening to her softly cry, before I answered. "I'm scared of everything, Lauren," I said.

I think she heard me, but she didn't say another word.

# November 20

A couple of days have passed since I last wrote in this thing. I've been here for two weeks, and already I'm swamped with homework. Hideous math stuff, mostly. That's one thing I'll say about Lauren. She's a real whiz at math. If you sweet-talk her long enough, you can con her into giving you most of the answers.

We've kind of gotten used to each other. Secretly, I still don't like her much, of course. But compared to everyone else here, I'll take Lauren. At least she despises Hopeless as much as I do. She's a real disappointment to everybody, I think. Just like me. For one thing, she still barely touches her food. Now and then she'll eat a few vegetables, but that's about it. Last night she ate three whole green beans and everybody acted like it was a real breakthrough.

And she'll even help me be disruptive, I've discovered. Today, for example, we got kicked out of our relaxation-therapy class. They're supposed to be teaching us how to relax in stressful situations.

Andrea was doing guided imagery, where we imagine we're in a place that makes us feel peaceful. She had us floating on these nice imaginary clouds. But then one thing led to another, and my cloud somehow turned into a marshmallow. I started to mentally munch it, and when I told Lauren what was happening, she started laughing uncontrollably. They sent us to our room to meditate on our sins.

So there we were. I was working on this endless story problem about trains going different directions at different speeds. Lauren was cutting pictures of skinny models out of fashion magazines. She has a whole collection. She puts them in order, according to skinniness. Apparently thigh size is a big factor in her decision-making. I know Sarge and the others don't approve of her behavior, but they just ignore it. I guess it's pretty common. Kendra had this big pinup of Twiggy on her bathroom door for a long time, and they never said anything. Eventually she took it down, all on her own.

I don't see what the big deal is. I used to keep a picture of myself taped on the refrigerator to remind me of how awful I looked in one of my heavier phases. It's basically the same thing. And anyway, what's so wrong with trying to be thin? The world revolves around thin people. Just look at any magazine. Turn on any TV show. Look at all the diet ads. It's not my fault the world wants you to be skinny. That's just the way it is, and

Lauren and I are only trying to follow the rules.

So anyway, we were sitting there on our beds, when all of a sudden I looked up and there were these two cute—I mean awesomely cute—guys standing in the doorway. I recognized one as Justin Davis, an eighth-grader on the basketball team. I'd never seen the other guy before. He was short, a few inches shorter than I am. But he had these great green eyes and a nice smile.

Naturally, I did what any red-blooded American girl would do under the circumstances. I dove under my covers, pretending to be asleep.

"Hi, Lauren," Justin said. I know it was him because I peeked over my sheet to check.

"Justin!" Lauren tossed her cut-out skinny girls aside. She sounded terrified. I considered coming out of my cocoon to rescue her, but I think I was even more terrified than she was. Besides, they clearly weren't here to see me. I happen to be invisible to guys—seriously, they never notice me. It's quite a unique talent, actually. I may go on *Star Search* with it.

"I, uh, I brought you these." Justin held out a box of chocolates.

Lauren looked horrified. For my part, I started salivating.

"This is Daniel Byrne," Justin said. "He just moved here from Ohio. He's going to be trying out for the team."

"What can I say?" Daniel said. "I'm an optimist."
I guess he was referring to his height. I wanted to
point out there were plenty of short players in the
Basketball Hall of Fame, but I kept my mouth shut.
Not only do guys not see me, they don't hear me
either.

Lauren sat there, barely moving. I think she was
terrified Justin was going to offer her a chocolate.

"Is your roommate asleep?" Justin asked in a
whisper.

"Zibby, are you asleep?" Lauren called.

"Yes."

"She's asleep, all right," Lauren confirmed.
"That's Zibby Lloyd, by the way."

"Oh, yeah," Justin said. "She's in our English
class, right? What's wrong with her?"

I couldn't believe he hadn't already heard.
South Somerset's not exactly a huge school. Of
course, we traveled in different circles. Justin and
Lauren were in the preppy/class leader/jock/model
student circle. I hung with a slightly smaller
crowd of one—me.

"Zibby, uh, has—" Lauren hesitated. I couldn't
believe she wasn't going to tell. Suddenly I liked
her a whole lot more.

I had to act quickly. I peered over my sheet. "I
have amnesia."

okay, so maybe I lied. I don't even know what
made me think of amnesia. Wait. Yes, I do. I'd seen

it on a soap opera Kendra was watching in the recreation room yesterday. This married woman named Tempest got amnesia, then married a new guy, then remembered she was already married. Something like that. The fine points were sort of lost on me.

"You mean you don't remember anything?" Justin asked. He seemed rather impressed.

I sneaked a peek at Lauren. She was still looking at the chocolates. My little white lie hadn't even seemed to sink in.

"Well, bits and pieces," I replied.

"Cool," Justin said. "What a great way to get out of doing homework."

"How did it happen?" Daniel asked. He was staring at me intently. I couldn't be sure if he bought my story or not. Justin seemed to, though. Which didn't exactly surprise me. Just because he had a great hook shot didn't mean he was a genius *off* the court.

"Happen?" I repeated. I had that queasy feeling I always get when my lies start spinning out of control. My mind was racing. How had Tempest gotten amnesia? She'd been pushed down an elevator shaft by her evil twin. Nope. That was a little melodramatic.

"The truth is, I—"

"She doesn't like to talk about the car accident, Justin," Lauren interrupted in a hushed tone.

Bless her perfect little devious mind. Maybe I'd misjudged Lauren.

"Sorry," Justin muttered.

Daniel walked over to my bed. His eyes were the color of green Jell-O. A gross comparison, maybe, but I happen to love green Jell-O. I crouched a little lower under my sheet and wondered if there was a subtle way I could hide the zit on my chin. Covering my head with the blanket seemed a little obvious.

"So, you're saying you don't remember anything about your past?" Daniel asked.

I paused a minute. There was an actual, certifiable male standing less than twenty-four inches away from me. Talking to me, no less. Maybe I was visible, after all. So much for *Star Search*.

"Well, I remember some things," I said. "Like my dog Charlie. He died when I was eight. We had to have him put to sleep when he ate our entire Thanksgiving turkey while it was defrosting." Come to think of it, maybe bingeing ran in the family.

Daniel laughed. "Do you remember anything else?"

I shrugged. "My times tables. But only through fourteen."

He laughed again, even harder. He had a very nice laugh, I decided.

Lauren cleared her throat. "Zibby really needs her rest, guys."

"Yeah, well, we should get going anyway," Justin said. "Hey, I almost forgot." He unzipped his backpack. "I brought your camera back. Thanks for letting me borrow it."

"You can hang on to it. I won't be needing it here," Lauren said quietly.

"But—" Justin hesitated. "Well, your mom, uh, said she wanted you to have it. I guess your doctor thought it would be good therapy."

Lauren rolled her eyes. "I don't need therapy. I need to get out of here, is all."

Justin placed the camera on the nightstand. "But you're so good. How about those pictures you took at the gymnastics meet?" Justin insisted. "Ms. Campbell says you have a great eye." Ms. Campbell teaches art and photography at our school.

"I'm terrible." Lauren shook her head adamantly.

"You're perfect at everything else," I pointed out, with more than a little bitterness. "You're undoubtedly a perfect photographer, too."

"Could we just *drop* this, please?" Lauren cried, her voice wavering. "Justin, I really think you should go now."

Justin chewed on his lower lip. "Lauren, I—I wanted to ask you about—" He looked over at Daniel and me, like he expected us to leave, but I had no intention of missing the good stuff. This was as close as I'd ever gotten to intimate coed conversation.

"About the Christmas dance," he finished in a rush. "I know it's a long way away—"

"Justin, please," Lauren moaned. "I don't want to talk about it, not now."

"okay," Justin said quietly. "It can wait. But I won't go with anybody but you." He reached over and took her hand. Lauren tried to pull away, but he held on tightly. It was, in my estimation, a supremely romantic moment.

"There's something else," he said. "You know that cousin of mine I told you about? Cassie? The one who was an anorexic?"

"Justin!" Lauren cried. She yanked her hand free. "Will you please just *go*?"

I looked over at Daniel, who looked back at me and shrugged helplessly. What could I do?

"I talked to Cassie about you, Lauren, and she told me you have to believe that you'll get better. It takes a long time, and it's really hard. But you can get better, Lauren. I know you can."

Lauren leaned her head back on her pillow and closed her eyes. Justin brushed her thin, tangled hair with his hand. "Come on, Daniel," he said, nodding at the door. "Let's get moving."

Daniel smiled at me. Great smile. Nice teeth. "Eleven times fourteen," he said.

"One fifty-four," I replied.

"Not bad," he said. "There's hope for you yet."

He followed Justin to the door. "Hey," I said.

"Good luck with the basketball."

"Thanks," Daniel said. "I'll probably need it."

"Muggsy Bogues is only five feet four, and he's in the NBA."

Daniel laughed. "How'd you remember that?"

Oops. "It's a medical miracle," I said lamely. "Suddenly I can remember sports trivia, too."

I could hear him laughing all the way down the hall. A nice laugh, though. I had the feeling he was laughing *with* me. Not *at* me, which is usually the case.

"Justin is gorgeous," I said. "I think he really has the hots for you."

Lauren opened her eyes and turned to me. There were tears running down her cheeks.

"Hey, why are you bawling?" I asked. "Most of the girls in our class would love to be in your shoes."

"I've known Justin since I was nine," Lauren said softly. "We've always been friends. I could tell him anything, Zibby. But now, all of a sudden, he wants things to change. Being friends isn't enough anymore. He wants me to be his *girl*friend."

"So?" I couldn't exactly see the problem. I was the Amazing Invisible Woman around guys, and Lauren had the most desirable male in Somerset drooling all over her. As far as I could see, I was the one who should be bawling. Strangely, though, I didn't feel as jealous as I should have. I was still thinking about Daniel's green Jell-O eyes.

"I just don't see why things have to change," Lauren said. "Why can't they stay the same? Remember how simple everything was before we got to middle school? Why can't it be like that forever?" She let out a deep sigh. "I just want to be able to control things better, you know?"

Did *I* know? I was the one who went on wild food binges. She was the one with the amazing self-control. The one who could overcome desperate hunger and refuse to eat a morsel of food. "It seems to me you have a lot of control over your life," I said. "A whole lot more than me, anyway."

"But I don't. Not yet," Lauren said, a desperate edge to her voice. "If I'm just a little stronger, maybe then . . ." Her voice trailed off.

*If I'm just a little stronger.* How many times had I said that as the need to go on a binge overtook me? Suddenly I realized that Lauren and I were really after the same thing. We just wanted to get our lives under control. She did it one way, by not eating. I did it another, by using food like a drug, to stop me from thinking about things that made me unhappy. Things like the fact that I was invisible to guys. And that I always would be. I was fat and ugly and that was that.

Sarge peeked into the door. "I think I'll just take those for safekeeping, sweetie," she said. She walked over and picked up the box of chocolates.

"Please, get them out of my sight," Lauren said. "You can have them if you want."

"You may change your mind later," Sarge said.

As I watched her whisk away the box, I thought my heart would break. Lauren didn't even seem to notice they were gone.

I looked over at her, and this time I didn't see how sick she was. I saw skinny, perfect, pretty little Lauren, was all. A girl that a guy like Justin went after. What did *she* have to complain about? It could be so much worse.

She could be me.

# November 24

I know, I know. It's been several days since I've even looked at this diary. I guess I'm not in the mood for it. What's the point? It's not going to change me. Nothing will change me. I've been here for almost three weeks and that's become pretty apparent.

There's only one solution. I've got to get out of here. I was doing better on my own.

Of course, Dr. P. would say that's negative thinking. She says how I *think* about things can change how I *feel* about things. She seems to think that I expect to fail here at Hopeless House.

The only person who hates it worse than I do here is Lauren. Unlike Lauren, I at least make a halfhearted attempt to do what they ask us to do. For example, I talk to my mom and dad in family sessions. We still argue all the time, but we're kind of getting used to it. It's like a new language. Instead of learning to speak French, we're learning to speak Fight.

Or when the EDs do role-playing in communications therapy, I go along with it. (Yesterday I played a mom who was criticizing her daughter. Kendra played my kid. She actually stood up for herself at one point—a real first for Kendra.) And I haven't binged since I got here. Not because I don't want to. Because they make it impossible.

But Lauren's another story. She's eating more because they don't give her any choice. Besides, I think in her heart she's still the good little girl who wants to please everybody. And I have to say she looks better as a result. She's still a walking toothpick, but at least there's a little color in her sunken cheeks. But when it comes to therapy, Lauren puts her foot down. She really doesn't want to change.

Neither do I, and I guess that's why we've started hanging around with each other more. It's crazy, I know, given the way I've always felt about her. But when the choice comes down to Lauren or someone else, I'll pick Lauren every time.

Naturally, the staff thinks we're a bad influence on the other kids. I'm used to being a bad influence, but it's definitely a new experience for Lauren.

Today was a perfect example. During group therapy, Andrea and Dr. P. brought in a camera and some special video equipment. They made all of us put on leotards. Then they took a picture of each of us standing in front of a wall, first sideways, then frontways.

That was bad enough. We all hate having our pictures taken. It's just a reminder of how ugly our bodies are. I hadn't worn a leotard since my ballet days. One look in the mirror and I knew why. My stomach bulges out like I'm five months pregnant, and my thighs are the size of tree trunks. Not a pretty picture. As for Lauren, it took her an hour to put the leotard on. She only did it because she knew if she refused, they'd take away her exercise privileges.

After they took our pictures, we got to change back into our clothes. Then we met in the therapy room. There was a big-screen TV there, hooked up to a computer. A woman named Lydia was sitting at the keyboard.

"I hope you're showing a horror movie," I said to Dr. P. "I just love a good scream now and then."

"Sorry, Zibby." Dr. P. shook her head. "No horror movies today. But I do think the ending of this presentation will shock most of you."

They turned out the lights, and Lydia pushed some buttons on the computer.

Silhouettes of several different girls appeared on the screen. They were all shapes and sizes. You could only see the outlines of their bodies. No faces. Tall, short, thin, medium, fat, really fat, really, really fat. You get the idea.

Each silhouette was numbered. "I want you each to pick the silhouette that's yours," Dr. P. said. "An outline of each of you will appear on the screen, but there are lots of other body types, too. See if you can pick your own."

Lydia ran them past us again and again. I finally decided that I was number seventeen. Not quite the fattest silhouette, but close to it. And seventeen had elephant thighs. I knew it had to be me.

Lauren picked number eighteen. Which was crazy, because eighteen had big thighs, a bigger rear, and no waist to speak of. It had been my second choice. But there was no way the silhouette belonged to Lauren.

We wrote our choices down on a piece of paper, along with our names, and gave them to Dr. P. She glanced them over, then handed them to Lydia.

"Now for the interesting part," Dr. P. said. "Lydia is going to place your actual silhouette next to the number you guessed was your own. Let's see how close you come. Who's first, Lydia?"

"Let's see." Lydia glanced down at the first piece of paper. "Zibby Lloyd."

Lucky me. We all sat there waiting expectantly. Suddenly a dark image flashed up on the screen. It was number seventeen. "That's me," I remarked. "Thunder thighs."

A few people giggled. "Now let's see the *real* Zibby Lloyd," Dr. P. said.

Another figure flashed onto the screen. Several girls gasped. Next to number seventeen, she looked like she'd lost about a third of the weight. She was nicely proportioned. Just about right, in fact. In other words, she wasn't me.

"No way that's me," I said forcefully. "Look at her thighs!" I stood up so the group could get a better look. "Now look at my thighs."

"But it is you," Dr. P. replied, smiling. "That's the whole point of this exercise. One of the biggest problems anorexics and bulimics face is their distorted image of their bodies. They look in the mirror and see something that really isn't there."

I stared at the screen in disbelief.

"Those *are* your thighs," Rachel remarked. "You're wrong, Zibby."

"Lydia, would you print out a copy of the silhouettes so Zibby can look them over?" Dr. P. asked.

A few seconds later, the computer printed out a copy of the figures on the screen. Dr. P. handed the page to me.

"How is it possible I could be that wrong?" I demanded skeptically. "It's not like I'm blind."

"A lot of us *are* blind, when it comes to our body image," Dr. P. responded. "And not just girls with eating disorders, either. Many of us want to live up to an unrealistic ideal. We're not satisfied unless we look like the models we see in magazines. I'll tell you a little secret. An awful lot of models have eating disorders just like you folks."

"But we really *are* fat," Kendra argued. "They aren't."

Dr. P. shook her head. "That's why we're doing this exercise, Kendra. The body you imagine you have is not the one you really have. Over time, you're going to learn to tell the difference." She sat down next to Kendra on the big stuffed couch. "But it's not just people with eating disorders who are unhappy with their looks. Ask any girl if she's content with her body the way it is, and she'll probably tell you no. Her nose is too big, or her breasts are too small, or she'd be perfectly happy if she could just lose another ten pounds. Instead of being at home in our bodies, we learn to hate them. We start to believe that if only our bodies were perfect, everything else in our lives would be perfect, too."

"But it's *true*," Lauren protested. I was kind of surprised to hear her say anything. She hardly ever spoke up during group.

"If you're not happy on the inside, it doesn't matter how the outside looks, Lauren. I know that's hard to accept, especially for girls. Boys sometimes get eating disorders, but ninety-five percent of the victims are female." Dr. P. stood and walked over to Lauren's side. "Let me ask you something, Lauren. You worry a lot about what other people say when they see you, don't you?"

"Well, sure," Lauren replied defensively. "Everybody does."

"What do you think they say when they look at you?"

Lauren stared at her hands. "That I'm ugly," she whispered. "And fat and repulsive. That I can't do anything right."

It was hard to believe, coming out of Little Ms. Perfect's mouth. How could she be so wrong about the way people perceived her? A thought hit me then like a bolt out of the blue. What if *I'm* wrong, too, about the way people perceive me? But no. I really *am* fat and ugly. Lauren's the one with delusions.

"How much time do you spend thinking about other people's looks, Lauren?" Dr. P. continued.

"Well, I notice how much skinnier they are than me. But mostly I think about my own weight."

Dr. P. nodded. "That's a mistake a lot of us make. We spend so much time thinking about ourselves, we assume the rest of the world is thinking about us, too. But I've got a big surprise for you. They're not. That cute boy you've got your eye on isn't thinking about your thighs. He's thinking about the pimple on his nose—the pimple you probably haven't even noticed, because you're so busy worrying about your thighs."

Dr. P. put her hand on Lauren's shoulder. "When you look at Zibby, what do you see, Lauren?"

Lauren looked at me. A smile formed on her lips.

"A crack-up," she said. "Someone who makes me laugh."

"Does she seem ugly to you?"

"No!" Lauren exclaimed in surprise. "Zibby's really cute."

Me, cute? Maybe the anorexia had damaged her eyesight.

"Zibby, when you look in the mirror, what do you see?"

I cleared my throat. "Um, well. . . let's just say 'cute' isn't one of the adjectives I would use."

Dr. P. stood up and looked at the group. "So who's right? Zibby, or Lauren? Do you see my point?"

A few girls nodded. Personally, the whole discussion was making me very uncomfortable. Visions of double-dark-chocolate-fudge cake kept dancing through my head—anything to take my mind off all these confusing thoughts. Why did Dr. P. have to go messing up our minds this way? I had it all figured out. I didn't want to have to *un*figure it.

"Lydia, let's see Lauren Kent's silhouette now," Dr. P. instructed.

Lauren shifted uncomfortably in her chair and shot me a desperate get-me-out-of-here look. Up on the screen came number eighteen, the figure Lauren had chosen as her own.

"There's who Lauren sees in the mirror," Dr. P. said.

Lydia flashed the actual image of Lauren's body on the screen. Everyone gasped.

"And there's the real Lauren," Dr. P. added.

It was astounding. The real Lauren was a tiny, painfully thin, stooped silhouette. She looked more like a stick figure than a human being. Next to her, number eighteen was easily three times the size.

"This is a trick!" Lauren cried. She leaped out of her chair.

"It's no trick, Lauren. Exactly the same thing happened to Zibby," Dr. P. said. "I know what a shock it is at first, hon. It's amazing how much we can distort reality."

"That is *not* me!" Lauren shouted. She ran to the TV and pounded on the screen. "I am fat, fat, fat!"

"Lauren," Dr. P. said in a soothing voice as she joined Lauren. "Everyone here knows just how you're feeling. It's scary to learn new ways of thinking about ourselves. That's why you're here, where it's safe to try them out."

"I hate it here!" Lauren whirled around and began pounding on Dr. P. "I hate you!"

Without thinking, I jumped out of my chair and ran to Lauren. I put my arm around her and led her toward the door. "Thank you, Zibby," Dr. P. said. "Why don't you two go back to your room now and get some rest?"

I nodded and led Lauren into the hall. I don't know why Dr. P. left us alone, but she did. It was probably just as well. I figured no one else but me knew how Lauren was really feeling.

"I hate them all, Zibby," she sobbed.

"I hate them, too," I said.

*Don't worry, Lauren. We're in this together*, I wanted to say. *We're friends.* But of course, I couldn't really say those words out loud. What if she laughed at me?

We walked slowly down the hall, number seventeen and number eighteen side by side, and didn't say another word.

# November 26

Today is a day that will go down in history. Today, with my clever and devious mind, I came up with a daring plan for my Great Escape. (I guess I should say *our* Great Escape, since, believe it or not, Lauren has decided to leave Hopeless with me.)

Ever since the video incident the other day, we've both been feeling pretty lousy about all the pressure they're putting on us to change. Even Rachel and Kendra have been giving us a hard time about getting with the program. But the harder they push, the more Lauren and I get angry. And the angrier we get, the more united we've become against the Enemy. The Enemy, we've decided, is just about everybody in the entire world, with the possible exception of Lauren's cat Bobo, since Bobo loves her no matter how much she weighs. (Charlie, my dog who ate the turkey, would have come under this category, too, except for his being deceased.)

Lauren even includes Justin on our Enemies list. He hasn't called or visited since the day he showed up here with Daniel. I think she's relieved. To tell the truth, for a while I was kind of hoping to see Daniel again. Of course, I know now that's crazy. What would he want with an ugly, fat amnesiac?

Anyway, today we were sitting around looking at pictures, when the idea of the Great Escape came to me. Ms. Kent brought in this big box of photographs Lauren had taken. Dr. P. thought it would be good for her to have them around as an incentive to start using her camera again. (They're big on creative outlets here. Unfortunately, my mouth is my only creative outlet. Although I did make an impressive pot holder in art therapy last week.)

Some of Lauren's photos were incredible. Of course, Lauren didn't believe me when I told her so, but they were. She'd taken all kinds of candid photos of people. A little homeless girl she saw one afternoon downtown. An old man holding hands with his grandson. There were even a few of Bobo, a very, very fat Siamese cat. But my favorites were some she'd taken of a gymnastics meet last year—the last one I'd attended, in fact. She caught all the energy and excitement and put it on film. But she also caught the dark side of competition. There was a picture of a little girl, an eight-year-old, crying bitterly when she fell during her floor routine. And there was even a picture of me, although I didn't remember Lauren taking it. It was after I'd really blown my balance-beam routine. I'd just seen my rotten score, and there's this look of utter futility in my eyes.

"Boy, do I look fat in my leotard," I said, gazing at the black-and-white photo.

"No, you don't," Lauren said. "You look great."

I shook my head. She was just being nice. "You can tell I really loved competing," I said sarcastically. "Check out the look of joy on my face."

"How about me?" Lauren asked, handing me another photo. Ms. Kent had taken it right before Lauren started her floor routine. "And talk about fat!"

I gazed at the photo. Even then, Lauren was painfully thin. "You got a great score on this routine, didn't you?"

Lauren scowled. "Who cares?"

I laughed in surprise. "Who cares? You got a gold medal in the state competition last year!"

Lauren frowned. "Wanna know something?" she whispered, glancing over at the door.

I nodded. I couldn't imagine what dark secret she was about to reveal.

"I don't exactly like gymnastics," Lauren admitted. She paused, as though she expected the roof to cave in. When it didn't, she smiled a little. "In fact, I don't like it at all," she said a little louder. "As a matter of actual fact, I *despise* it!" She clasped her hand over her mouth. "I can't believe I just said that, Zibby! I've *never* said that! I've never even let myself *think* it!"

I laughed. "It's all that talk in therapy about letting out your real feelings. I think it's starting to get to you."

Lauren chewed nervously on a fingernail. "I shouldn't have said that. If my mom ever heard me—"

"Yes, you should have said it. You have a right to your own feelings, Lauren."

"But gymnastics is so important to her."

"To your mom?"

Lauren nodded. "She used to be a gymnast herself. A good one. But she wants me to be even better. I try, really I do, but I'd rather . . ." She trailed off and glanced at the camera on her dresser.

"You'd rather take pictures?"

She nodded.

"Then you should quit gymnastics and work on your photography," I said logically. It's so easy solving other people's problems.

"Oh, I'll never be any good at photography," Lauren said quickly.

"What do you mean? You already *are*!"

"You want to know what I'm good at?" Lauren asked. Her voice had an angry edge I hadn't heard since the video incident. "I'm good at losing weight, Zibby. As a matter of fact, I'm great at it. It's the one thing I do really well, and they won't let me do it anymore." Tears formed in her eyes. "It was the only time I felt happy."

"Like when I was bingeing." I nodded. "If I could just get my hands on a little chocolate for an afternoon. I wouldn't have to lose control totally like I used to. Just a little bit, you know?"

Lauren smiled. "Don't forget the big Thanksgiving party Thursday. Maybe you could talk Ms. Brady into stuffing the turkey with Hershey bars!" She made a face. "I'm dreading it, aren't you? My parents always seem to have a fight during the holidays."

"Don't your parents get along?"

"Oh, sure," Lauren said quickly. "Of course they do. But everybody's parents fight."

"True." I nodded. "I've had a few arguments with mine in family sessions."

"What about?"

"I told them I thought they favored Cheryl and Brad. That I was always the disappointment." I shrugged. "Of course, they denied it. But it's true. I *am* a disappointment."

"Join the club."

"Let me tell you something. If your parents are disappointed in Little Ms. Perfect, they'd definitely want to disown me!"

"Little Ms. Perfect?" Lauren repeated. "You mean—"

"You, of course!"

Lauren laughed bitterly. "Not perfect enough, Zibby. Not by a long shot. Maybe it's because I'm an only child or something." She sighed. "I'm dreading Thursday. It'll be so weird, not having Thanksgiving at home. You know how it is. Usually you're all excited because school's out and you have four whole days of freedom——"

"Wait just a minute," I interrupted. "Suppose we *did* have our freedom, Lauren?"

"Dream on."

I jumped off her bed. Suddenly I was too excited to sit still. The more I thought about it, the more it made sense. "No, I'm serious, Lauren. Think about it. Thursday will be really chaotic around here. All the kids at Hopeless will have families visiting, and they're going to have the big party in the recreation room."

Lauren combed her fingers through what was left of her hair. "So?"

"So, what better time to make our getaway? In all the commotion, they won't notice we're gone for ages."

"But——but what would we do?"

"We'd be free!" I exclaimed. "What have you been wanting to do more than anything in the world?"

"Jog," Lauren answered instantly. "For miles. Without someone telling me I have to stop because it's bad for me."

"And all I want out of life is a couple candy bars," I said. The words alone were enough to make my mouth water. "And maybe a bite or two of ice cream, without someone telling me I can't trust myself."

"But what if we're caught?" Lauren asked.

I could see she didn't have my outlaw instincts. That was okay, though. You couldn't expect a perfect person to reform overnight. "That's part of the excitement, Lauren. Come on. Live dangerously for a change! Besides," I added, "if we want to, we'll come back later on, so our parents won't worry. Or better yet, maybe we'll just go straight home, and tell them we refuse to come back here. How about that?"

Lauren thought for a moment. "You mean we might never have to come back to this place?"

"Not if we don't want to. We don't belong here, Lauren. We're not like Rachel and Kendra and the others." I took a deep breath. All of a sudden I realized how much I wanted her to say yes. Not that I couldn't handle escaping on my own. But the company would be nice. It was easier fighting the Enemy when you had help. "What do you say?"

Lauren nodded slowly. "I say, let's bust out of this joint!" she said.

So it's decided. The Great Escape will be on Thursday. I'm counting the hours. At last, freedom. Freedom and food. Not a bad combination, if I do say so myself.

# November 28—Thanksgiving

It's eleven in the morning, and all systems are go. Lauren and I have the whole thing planned out. Some of the Hopeless volunteers and staff members are going to be putting on a little entertainment for the families this afternoon before turkey time. Alison Kim, this high school girl who's been volunteering at Hopeless ever since her little sister died of Hodgkin's disease, is going to sing songs and accompany herself on the guitar. (Look out, MTV.) Rumor has it Dr. Steve may even play a little piano number. That's almost worth sticking around for, but not quite.

It'll be the perfect time to make our getaway, we figure. Fortunately, we even have some cash, because Lauren's parents give her an outrageous allowance. (Note: this is an urgent topic to discuss with Mom and Dad as soon as possible.)

I can't wait. Freedom. Glorious freedom. No Calorie Cops. No rules. No nothing. Just Lauren and me, on our own.

I can already taste the chocolate.

# December 2

Four days have passed since I last wrote in this. Four long days. Today's the first day I've been strong enough to pick up a pen. It's hard to know where to start, so much has happened. But I guess I should begin at the beginning, with Thanksgiving Day.

Just as we'd hoped, things were chaotic around here that day. Everybody's families showed up, and the place was pretty festive, for a house full of sick people. My family was, as usual, perky. Lauren's parents were more tense. They hovered around her like she was a two-year-old. When they weren't hovering, they stood off in a corner and talked in low whispers to each other. Poor Lauren. I couldn't decide which was harder to take. My family, where everyone pretends we're so happy and well-adjusted we could be on a TV sitcom. Or her family, where you could cut the tension with a knife.

The volunteers and staff put on a talent show around noon. Everybody gathered in the recreation room on the bottom floor. Alison Kim was the first performer. When she launched into a stirring rendition of "Koom Bay Ya," I gave Lauren the thumbs-up signal.

"I'm freezing," Lauren whispered to her mother. "I'm going to go get another sweater."

"I'll go with you," I volunteered.

We sneaked out the door just as the whole room burst into song. When we made it upstairs, the hallway was deserted. We made a quick stop in our room so I could grab my backpack. We'd already stuffed our jackets, wallets, and toothbrushes in it.

Now came the tricky part. We had to make it back downstairs through the lobby without attracting any attention. "Ready?" I asked Lauren.

She looked even paler than usual. "As I'll ever be," she replied.

When we got downstairs, we could hear Alison. She was still singing the same song. "Doesn't that dumb song ever end?" I said under my breath. We walked down the hall toward the spacious lobby. Fortunately, the recreation room was at the far end of the house, so we wouldn't have to walk directly past it.

"Coast is clear," I whispered.

We tiptoed toward the door as fast as we could. Just as I put my hand on the knob, I heard footsteps behind me. "Going somewhere, ladies?" a male voice inquired.

I whirled around. It was Rusty Feller, a part-time nurse with bright red hair and tons of freckles. He was dressed in a clown costume—for the show, I assumed, but you never knew with Rusty.

Fortunately, I was prepared for just such an emergency. "We're looking for my little brother," I said quickly. "Brad. He's nine. Talks a mile a minute. Have you seen him?"

"Nope," Rusty said. "Want me to help you look?"

"Oh no," Lauren said quickly. "He's probably just roaming around the house exploring. And you don't want to miss the show."

Rusty tossed a ball into the air. It landed with a crash on a nearby lamp. "Hurry now," he said as he retrieved the ball. "My juggling act is next."

"You, juggling?" I asked. Rusty was a major league klutz. Even klutzier than me.

"Well, I'm still in training," Rusty admitted.

"We'll be there in a minute," I said as Rusty dashed off toward the recreation room.

"That was close," I murmured. "Let's hit the road while we still have the chance." I checked behind me one last time. Then I slipped out the door, with Lauren on my heels.

We ran across the lawn and down the block as fast as we could. Lauren was still a little shaky, so we stopped at the corner to catch our breath. The air was crisp and clear and the sidewalk was littered with dry leaves. "Isn't it beautiful?" I asked. "We're really free, Lauren!"

She nodded. "I'm going to run and run and

run until I can't go any farther."

I noticed that she was shivering. It *was* awfully cold. Colder than I'd expected. "Here." I unzipped my backpack and handed Lauren her windbreaker. "Put this on. You look like you're freezing."

"I am, a little. But it feels wonderful."

"Where to, first?" I asked. "You still want to go to the square?"

Lauren nodded. "Come on," she said. "I'll race you."

Somerset Square was only a few blocks away, in the center of the downtown shopping district. It was a little park that was perfect for people-watching or jogging. Unfortunately, there weren't very many people to watch, what with it being Thanksgiving and all. I hadn't really counted on that fact. Almost everything on the way to the square was closed, including Jane's Ice Cream Shop, one of my very favorite high-calorie hangouts. The 7-Eleven was open, of course, but I had a feeling they wouldn't be all that thrilled about having me stop by to reminisce about the good old days of shoplifting Krispy Kremes.

To my relief, we passed Konstas on the way, a little mom-and-pop convenience store that stays open 365 days a year. "I'm going to do a little shopping," I said, pausing in front of the store.

"Here," Lauren said. She reached into her pocket for her wallet and handed me a twenty-dollar bill. "It's on me."

"Do you want anything?"

"No, I'm not hungry."

I knew I should have expected that response. But I felt guilty, spending someone else's money on my binge. I was used to operating alone. I pressed the money back into Lauren's hand. "Maybe I should just, uh, *borrow* a few things."

"You mean shoplift?" Lauren hissed. She looked horrified.

For a moment there, I'd forgotten who I was dealing with. But who was Lauren to judge me? Her behavior wasn't exactly what you'd call normal.

Lauren handed me the money. "Take it," she pleaded. "My treat, Zibby, okay? I like to watch other people eat. Really. Do it as a favor for me."

I shrugged and went inside the store. Next time, maybe it would be easier to binge solo. Bingeing with an anorexic was a little like telling a dirty joke to your mother. It took all the fun out of it.

But pretty soon I forgot all about Lauren. All I could think of was the wonderland I'd just stepped into. I marveled at row after row of donuts and candy and cookies. Talk about Thanksgiving. I was definitely giving major thanks that the Konstas had decided to keep their store open on holidays.

I reminded myself that I was really only there to pick up a chocolate bar or two. Somewhere in my head I could hear Dr. P.'s words about food being like a drug—a drug that keeps us from feeling unpleasant things. Well, right now all I was feeling was a desperate need to taste some chocolate. And what was so wrong with that? Other girls could eat chocolate whenever they pleased without turning into monsters. Why couldn't I?

I picked up a basket and dropped a couple candy bars into it. My eye fell on the chocolate-chip cookies I'd loved since I was a child. I picked up two bags of those, too. Didn't I deserve them? Hadn't I been suffering through day after miserable day of lima beans and fruit salad?

As I stalked the aisles, grabbing anything that caught my eye, that familiar feeling came over me. It was as if I were in a dream, as if I didn't really exist. Nothing mattered but the dizzy excitement I was feeling. It was wonderful. It had been way too long since I'd felt this way.

When my basket was full, I carried it to the register. "You must be having company," the clerk said as she rang up my purchase.

"What? Oh, yeah. Lots of it," I lied. "A big party."

"Thirty-one dollars and fourteen cents, please."

I stared at the twenty in my palm as a wave of panic passed through me. How could I have spent that much? "Are—are you sure?" I stammered. "It didn't seem like that much."

She showed me the register tape. "See? Thirty-one fourteen. It really adds up, doesn't it?"

I handed her the twenty. "Can you hold on just a sec? I need to borrow the rest from my friend." I dashed out the front door. Lauren was jogging in place on the sidewalk. Her eyes had a glazed, far-away look.

"Lauren," I said frantically. "I need more money." I wasn't even embarrassed. I was past embarrassment. All I wanted was to eat, and if I'd had to steal the money from Lauren, I probably would have.

"Sure," she said indifferently. She reached for her wallet and tossed it to me, jogging all the while. "Take it all, I don't care."

I didn't even thank her. I just ran back inside and dropped another twenty on the counter. I almost forgot my change, I was so anxious to plunge into that bag of goodies.

"Enjoy your party," the clerk called.

"Oh, I will," I replied. "Trust me."

Lauren was right where I'd left her, jogging with gusto. "Let's go," I ordered, charging ahead.

She ran beside me as I tore open a bag of cookies with my teeth. I stuffed my mouth full of cookies and savored the sweet chocolate flavor. It was heavenly. I'd almost forgotten how heavenly. "Want one?" I asked.

Lauren looked aghast. "No!" she exclaimed. "I couldn't!"

"Suit yourself." It was just as well. There'd be that much more for me.

"I'm going to jog ahead," Lauren said as we

crossed the street. "I'll go around the park a few times. Where will I find you?"

"That bench near the fountain," I replied, dribbling cookie crumbs.

"See ya," Lauren called over her shoulder as she rushed off.

I watched her jog away and felt strangely relieved. I was used to bingeing privately. Having an audience took all the fun out of it. Not that I was particularly self-conscious. By the time I made it to the bench, I was ripping open bags and boxes like someone who hadn't seen food in a month. And in a way, I hadn't. Not food I cared about. Food that let me stop being me for a while.

I was on my second bag of ranch-style potato chips when a policewoman walked slowly by. I didn't even notice her until she was looming right over me.

"Hi," I said nervously. Had she been sent by the Hopeless people? I wondered. By now our parents had undoubtedly noticed that we were gone.

"Hungry?" she asked, smiling.

I shrugged, trying to look casual, which is difficult when you're drooling potato chips. "I just got off this killer diet, and I'm sort of celebrating."

She nodded. "Oh, my, do I know that feeling! I've been on every diet in the book. Fortunately, this job helps me walk off a few calories."

"Cookie?" I asked, remembering my manners.

"No, thanks." She peered at me more closely. "You going home after this?"

"Uh-huh. My grandma and grandpa are coming in from Toledo."

That was a good move on my part. Just as I'd hoped, the mention of grandparents seemed to reassure her. "Well, have a nice Thanksgiving. And don't get too carried away there."

I let out a sigh of relief as she headed on. For a moment I thought of my parents. They were probably frantically roaming the halls of Hopeless, worried sick. But that wasn't my problem. Not now. My problem was which to eat next: the chocolate-covered donuts or the Almond Joys. Nothing else mattered. Not them, not me, not anything.

Lauren jogged up after her first circle of the park. "This is great," she said breathlessly. "I'm free, Zibby! And think of the calories I've burned off!"

"Are you sure you're okay?" I asked as I unwrapped another candy bar. "You look a little pale."

Lauren did a couple deep-knee bends. "Are you kidding? I haven't felt this great in ages!" Her eyes dropped to the tangle of bags and crumbs at my feet. She seemed a little shocked, but I didn't care. She had her way of dealing with things. I had mine.

"Hey, what's seven times fourteen?" someone yelled.

My heart dropped a few feet. It was a boy's

voice, a familiar voice. *Daniel?*

"Look," Lauren said. "In the car at the red light."

Daniel was waving out of the rear window of a Honda packed with people. Probably family, it looked like. I waved halfheartedly. Then I shoved my bag of goodies under the bench while discreetly wiping my mouth on my sleeve.

The light changed and the car pulled over to the curb in front of us. Daniel leaned out the window. "You guys are out already?" he asked doubtfully.

"Thanksgiving," I said quickly. "They let us all out for the holiday, just like school."

Daniel nodded. I couldn't really tell if he was convinced. The other people in the car seemed to be staring at us doubtfully. "How's your memory?" he asked.

"Better. I can multiply up to my sixteens."

The man in the front seat said something to Daniel. "Gotta go," Daniel said. "We're heading over to my aunt's. You guys need a lift?"

"My mom's picking us up here in a few minutes," I lied.

"Hey, does this mean you'll be out for Christmas vacation, too?" Daniel asked.

Wasn't he ever going to leave? "Depends," I answered noncommittally.

"I was just thinking . . . oh well, never mind." He stared at me for another long second. Then the car started to pull away. "You forgot to tell me the answer," Daniel called.

"Ninety-eight," I yelled, but the car had already turned the corner.

"That was close," I mumbled as I reached for a handful of chips.

Lauren didn't answer. She had slumped onto the bench next to me. Her skin was gray and clammy. "You okay?" I asked.

She nodded. "Just a little tired. I was thinking, Zibby. Do you suppose our parents are very worried?"

Lauren really wasn't proving to be a reliable binge partner. The first rule of bingeing was that you didn't think about unpleasant things, like, for example, worried parents. I took a bite out of an oatmeal raisin cookie. "Look, we'll call them in a little while, if you want, okay?"

Lauren nodded slowly. I looked at her more closely and felt an annoying twinge of worry. She really didn't look too hot. She'd probably overdone it on the running. "Maybe we should go somewhere," I suggested. "You still have some money, right?"

"Lots."

"There's a cafeteria around the corner that might be open," I said. "Let's try that. It'll be warm, and you can get some hot tea or something." *And I can get some fried chicken or something*, I added to myself. "Plus there'll be a phone if we decide to call."

I stood up, and a thick layer of crumbs fell off of me like a blizzard. Lauren was so weak, I had to help her stand. We walked very slowly to the cafeteria. Lauren was really dragging, and I, of course, was still gorging on the remains of my goodie bag.

The cafeteria was open, fortunately. It was dimly lit and smelled like boiled vegetables. To my surprise, almost every table was full, most of them with just one person. There were a lot of very old people and a few families that looked very poor.

Instead of the anticipation I usually felt at the sight of yards and yards of food, I felt a horrible sadness descend on me. These people didn't have families who loved them like Lauren and I did. They couldn't afford turkey with all the trimmings—the stuff we took for granted. The stuff waiting for us back at Hopeless.

But I wasn't there to feel rotten and guilty. I was there to *stop* feeling that way. I led Lauren to a table, since she still seemed wobbly. "Want anything?" I asked.

She shook her head.

"Come on," I urged. "How about some tea?"

"okay," she agreed reluctantly. "And if they have it, some diet Jell-O."

"That's it?"

She handed me her wallet. "That's it."

I got a tray and stood in line. I tried very hard

not to notice the hunched-over old woman standing in front of me. She kept staring longingly at the food I piled high on my tray, but all she got for herself was a roll and a cup of coffee.

As we waited in line at the cashier, my eyes fell on the old woman's nearly empty tray. Maybe she wasn't very hungry, I told myself. She'd probably already had Thanksgiving dinner.

I paid for my food—another whopping twenty bucks—and headed for the table where Lauren sat waiting. My mouth was watering at the mound of mashed potatoes on my plate, but I couldn't seem to concentrate the way I usually do when I'm bingeing. Other feelings kept crowding my head. Guilty feelings. Worried feelings. Feelings I usually didn't allow myself to have.

Suddenly I stopped and spun around. I turned back toward the table where the old woman had just settled. "I don't know what came over me," I said. My words tumbled out before I knew what I was going to say. "I guess my eyes were bigger than my stomach, and now I've bought all this food . . . I don't suppose you could help me out?" Before she could answer, I started unloading food onto her tray—turkey, potatoes, vegetables, dessert. Lots of it.

"Gracious," she said, "I'll never eat all this, dear. But thank you. This is quite a little Thanksgiving you've cooked up for me. I don't know how to thank you."

I picked up my tray without a word and headed for Lauren. There was still enough food left for a major binge. And my stomach was already swollen to the point of bursting. I guess that's what happens when you don't stay in practice.

"Who was that?" Lauren asked as I handed her a cup of tea.

"I don't know, but you just bought her dinner out of the kindness of your heart." I looked up. "How're you feeling?"

"Lots better. I was just so cold, you know?" She stared at my plate. "You're really going to eat all that?"

"Where there's a will, there's a way."

She smiled, but it was a nervous-looking smile. "Zib, maybe you should slow down a little," she said.

"Hey, you forget I'm a pro," I replied. I didn't care what Lauren thought. I had mashed potatoes to contend with. I shoveled some food into my mouth while she watched in quiet amazement. My stomach had begun to ache, but I was used to that. "Don't look so shocked," I said with a shrug. "You're looking at someone who once cleaned out the entire contents of her parents' pantry in one sitting."

"We're really opposites, aren't we?" Lauren observed wryly. "Like mirror images. It's funny that we've ended up being friends."

Hearing the F word out loud took me for a loop. "Friends?" I repeated, trying not to sound hopeful. After all, Lauren had so many friends. What did she need with me?

"You're the first person I've ever felt I could just open up to and admit how I was really feeling," Lauren said. She took a careful sip of tea as I forced a roll into my mouth.

"Me too," I admitted, my mouth still full. "You know, I have a confession to make, Lauren. I used to really hate your guts."

Lauren's mouth dropped open. "You hated me? Why?"

"Well, maybe *hate's* a little strong. But I didn't like you much. Because you were perfect. And because I wasn't."

Lauren sighed. "But I'm not," she said softly. "You know that now."

I stopped eating long enough to look her in the eyes. They were wet with tears. "Yeah, I know that now," I said. "And you know what else? I like you now, too. Because you're human, like the rest of us."

Lauren smiled. "Human, huh? I kind of like the sound of that."

Just then I felt a sharp cramp in stomach. Not surprising, given its swollen size. I'd already unzipped my jeans and untucked my shirt to make extra room. Suddenly I knew I had to purge, and do it quickly. "I have to go to the bathroom," I told Lauren.

"Want me to come?" she asked.

"No!" I cried. The very thought of her seeing me that way terrified me. It was bad enough having a witness to my binge. I shoved back my chair and ran for the bathroom, holding up my jeans with one hand.

In the safety of the last stall, I leaned over the toilet. Panic came over me. What if I couldn't throw up? It had been so long since I'd done it. I probed my throat with my fingers for several minutes before I could start myself gagging. Then it began—the slow, awful, familiar vomiting.

Suddenly I felt a horrifying pain deep in my throat, a pain like nothing I'd ever felt before. Another wave of vomiting convulsed my body, and the pain doubled. It was as though my throat were splitting in two.

What was happening to me? This wasn't like all the other times. There was something terribly wrong. I tried to call for help, but all that came out was a strangled choking sound. Then something else came out. Deep red blood, waves and waves of it.

I sank to the cold floor and watched the ceiling grow black. I knew I was dying. And the strange thing was, I felt relieved.

# December 3

I couldn't write any more yesterday. I guess I was just too tired. They say surgery takes a lot out of you.

It turned out I had what they call an "esophageal tear." It happens to bulimics sometimes, when they vomit so hard it actually rips open the tube leading from the mouth to the stomach. If Lauren hadn't found me and called Hopeless House, the doctors say I could have bled to death. But she did, and they sewed me back up just in time. It hurts like crazy, and it'll be days before I can even touch solid food. But I'm alive. And I owe it all to Lauren.

She was the first person I saw when I woke up from surgery that night. My mom and dad were there, too, both of them crying. But it was Lauren I looked at first.

She was sitting next to my bed holding my hand. I tried to talk, but my throat felt as if someone were squeezing it shut with a vise. "Don't try to talk, honey," my mom said softly.

"The doctors say you're going to be fine, Zib," my dad added. "Just fine." He cleared his throat and sniffled. I'd never seen my dad cry before. I thought dads only cried in TV movies. "Of course," he added, "you won't be able to talk for a couple of days. Lauren'll like that, huh, Lauren?"

I managed a smile for my dad's benefit.

"Could I talk to Zibby alone?" Lauren asked. "For just a moment?"

After my parents left, Lauren stared at me hard. Tears fell freely down her cheeks. "You scared me to death, Zibby Lloyd," she said. "I found you in that pool of blood and I was so sure . . ." Her voice faded away. "And then—I have to tell you this, okay? Because it shows just what a rotten person I really am—"

I squeezed her hand to make her stop, but she shook her head. "No, really. When you hear this, you'll understand. I found you there in the bathroom, and for a moment I didn't know what choice to make. If I called the doctors, I knew I'd end up back here. And that made me so afraid that I almost wanted to leave you there, Zibby." A huge sob racked her frail body. "And then I thought, *What am I thinking? What kind of monster have I turned into, that I would let my friend die just to spare myself?* And I knew, I really knew it had gone too far."

I wanted to say I understood, but all I could do

was squeeze her hand extra tight. Lauren sighed. "So now you know. I don't deserve to be your friend, Zib." She wiped away a tear with the back of her hand. "But no matter what you decide, you've got to promise me one thing."

I nodded again.

"When I saw you lying there," Lauren said slowly, "it was like I saw you as you really were for the first time. You were lying there, all white, in a pool of blood and vomit, and all of a sudden what you were doing to yourself wasn't okay anymore. And I looked in the mirror and I sort of saw myself for the first time, too." She laughed ruefully. "And I think maybe I could afford to put on a pound or two, if you know what I mean. What I'm trying to say is, you have to try to get better now, Zibby. We tried fighting the Enemy, but I didn't know we could die fighting. And I'm starting to think maybe you and I are the *real* enemy. Know what I mean? Besides," she added with a smile, "I didn't drag my behind back here for nothing. I made the ultimate sacrifice for you, Zibby Lloyd. I'm going to be forced to eat Hopeless House meals again! And if I can eat Ms. Brady's meat loaf, you can promise me you'll get better."

I laughed, even though it hurt so much I wanted to cry.

"So, deal?" Lauren continued. "We both get better now? It'll be like one of those contracts we sign with Dr. P." She grinned. "Only, this one we're going to honor."

I squeezed her hand and drifted back to sleep. It was the first time in years I'd slept through the night without dreaming of food.

# December 14

Today I said something pretty amazing to Dr. P. Something I never dreamed I'd ever actually hear myself say—"I think I'm getting better."

"Why do you say that?" she asked, smiling.

"I looked in the mirror today, and for the first time I can ever remember, I did not say, 'You're ugly.'"

"What *did* you say when you looked in the mirror?"

"I said, 'You're not so bad, Zibby Lloyd.'" I rolled my eyes. "I couldn't exactly say 'You're the next Miss America, Zibby Lloyd.' That would have been pushing it a bit, don't you think?"

Dr. P. leaned back in her big leather chair and laughed. She had a very nice laugh, I'd decided. It reminded me a little bit of Daniel's.

It turned out that after he'd seen Lauren and me at the park Thanksgiving Day, Daniel had decided something seemed kind of fishy. He'd called Hopeless and talked to Dr. P. By that time, most of the staff was out searching for us.

Two weeks had passed since then, and Justin and Daniel hadn't called or stopped by. I guess we'd scared them off. Who could blame them? Besides, it wasn't like I'd ever *really* expected to see Daniel again. All we'd done was talk for a few minutes—not exactly a lifetime commitment on his part.

"I think you're getting better, too," Dr. P. said, shaking me from my thoughts of Daniel.

"Lots of people are," I agreed. I pulled my knees up to my chest and snuggled into her couch. She has this big comfy white sofa in her office with lots of colorful pillows on it. They're very convenient when you're feeling mad and you want to throw something without causing major damage. "Look how much better Kendra seems," I pointed out. "She's taking some kind of drug, isn't she?"

"An antidepressant," Dr. P. said. "Sometimes drug therapy is very helpful for people with eating disorders. Every person is different."

"Well, she looks a lot healthier." I smiled. "And she's definitely more assertive. I even heard her tell Rachel to mind her own business the other day. I couldn't believe my ears! But the biggest change is in Lauren," I added happily. "Don't you think?"

"She's improved a great deal," Dr. P. agreed.

"A great deal? She's like a different person! She's eating almost all her meals, she's put on some weight, and she's running all over Hopeless taking pictures of everybody she can find." I shook my finger at Dr. P. "That was a good idea of yours, suggesting she work on her photography. She took this picture of Spencer—you know the little boy with bone cancer?—that's amazing." I sighed. "Of course, try telling that to Lauren. She never believes me when I tell her how good she is."

"Have you ever wondered why Lauren's such a perfectionist?" Dr. P. asked.

"You tell me. You're the shrink."

Dr. P. pursed her lips thoughtfully. A lot of times she doesn't say anything. She just lets you sit there and stew and figure things out on your own. I think maybe I'll become a psychiatrist someday. Talk about your laid-back job.

"I guess Lauren's afraid of failing," I finally said. "She doesn't want to let anybody down."

Dr. P. nodded. "When you're afraid of failing, there are lots of ways people cope. Some people, like Lauren, try to do everything just right. Others don't try at all. They behave in self-destructive ways instead. That way, no one can say they tried and failed. If you never really try, you never really fail."

I stared out the window at the snow-covered garden. "You're talking about me, aren't you?"

"What do you think?"

"I think you sure ask a lot of questions," I said.

Dr. P. just smiled.

I cleared my throat. "You mean, like mouthing off in school."

"You, mouthing off?" Dr. P. teased.

"Or like shoplifting, things like that."

"Sometimes we act in a certain way because we think in all-or-nothing terms. We say, I'm either good, or I'm bad, and that's the role I'll always have to play. What do you think your role is in your family?"

I tossed a green pillow across the floor. Like I said, the pillows are a very good idea. "I'm the garbage disposal," I joked.

Dr. P. smiled, but I could see she was waiting for another answer. She's a very patient waiter, too. She'll wait all day if she has to.

"Well, I'm also kind of the troublemaker." I chewed on a thumbnail. "Brad's the perfect little baby, and Cheryl's the perfect big sister, and, well, you know. There's no room left for me."

But even as I spoke, I could see Dr. P.'s point. Maybe if I wasn't afraid of failing, I could try out a new role. Something a little more challenging. After all, I'd pretty much perfected the role of troublemaker. And my detention record would probably remain untouched for all time.

"I see what you mean, I think," I said. "Maybe I'm ready for the new, improved Zibby Lloyd."

"I think she's already made an appearance."

"You know something, Dr. P.?" I said softly.

"You know why I'm finally getting better?"

"Why?"

"Because Lauren and I made a contract of our very own. We didn't sign it or write it up or anything. But we promised each other we'd get better."

"That was a very smart thing for the two of you to do."

"You're not mad? After all, we kept breaking our contracts with you."

"Of course I'm not mad. I'm glad for you. Sometimes it takes a while to find the contract that works." She leaned forward, her chin cupped in her hand. "But you'll be going home soon, and I want you both to remember that it's okay to make mistakes. Everybody does. Recovery doesn't happen overnight. There are going to be times when you don't think you can ride through a craving for a binge. You may even break down and fall back into your old patterns. But that's okay, as long as you keep trying. Changing the way your mind thinks is like learning to use a new muscle. You have to practice at it every single day."

"We're not going to fail," I said confidently.

Dr. P. shook her head. "Did you hear what I said, though?"

"Yeah, I heard. But I have to think positively, right? You're the one who taught me about negative thinking."

"There's negative thinking. Then there's realistic thinking. I want you to know you're still a good person even when you make a mistake."

I laughed. "You're such a worrywart, Dr. P. Chill out."

What Dr. P. didn't understand was that I'd made enough mistakes for a lifetime. I wasn't going to waste time making any more.

# December 20, 12:10 A.M.

What an interesting day it's been. Well, interesting doesn't quite do it justice. Amazing, stupendous, incredible. No, that doesn't quite do it justice, either.

It all started this morning. When I got back to our room after my therapy session with Dr. P., Lauren was waiting there. "Justin called me today," she informed me.

"I thought he'd given up on you."

"Me too. I was hoping he had." She smiled wistfully. "But then, as soon as I heard his voice, I realized how much I'd missed him."

"What did he want?"

She reached for her brush and stared into her dresser mirror. "To ask me about the Christmas dance one last time. It's tonight, you know."

I'd completely forgotten. I usually block social events like that out of my mind, since I'm never invited. "So what did you tell him?" I asked. "I'll bet Dr. P. would let you out for the night, if you begged and pleaded."

"I said no," Lauren answered stiffly. "I told you, Zib. I don't want Justin to think of me that way." She sat on her bed and sighed. "At least, I *think* that's what I want. Or don't want." She cast me a desperate look. "What *do* I want, anyway? Can't you give me some useful advice?"

"Me, give advice on guys?" I groaned. "You might as well ask me about brain surgery. Still, since you asked . . . I suppose you could try taking it real slow with Justin. Maybe your friendship doesn't have to change, Lauren."

"Too late now. I think I really hurt his feelings." She shrugged. "He'll probably ask someone else to the dance. Tara Walters, maybe."

"The one with the mega-breasts?"

Lauren giggled. "She wears a triple-F bra, everyone says."

I climbed onto my bed and leaned back against my pillow. "I wonder who Daniel's going with," I said, trying to sound casual.

"When he asked me about the dance, Justin said he was hoping we could double with Daniel. But he didn't mention who he was taking."

*Zibby, you idiot*, I chided myself. Of course a guy like Daniel would be going to the dance with some perky cheerleader-type. With those eyes, it probably hadn't taken him long to hook up with someone.

"Justin did say he might stop by tonight,"

Lauren said hopefully. "Maybe that means he won't ask anyone else to the dance, after all."

"It's awfully late to be asking someone," I pointed out. "Only the real losers like me are left by this time."

Lauren shook her finger at me. "Zibby, you are *not*—"

"I know, I know," I said quickly. "Just a little slip. I am not a loser. Of course, I am not going to the dance, either. But I am not a loser."

"Would you have wanted to go?" Lauren asked.

"Depends. With Raymond Kropac, for example, no."

"The guy who keeps a gerbil in his shirt pocket?"

"You grasp my point. On the other hand—" There was no reason to name names. "Maybe with someone else I'd feel differently."

"But don't guys *scare* you?"

"To death. But that might be because I don't really know any."

"Well, this whole thing doesn't matter, since I doubt Dr. P. would have let me go to the dance anyway."

"We're going home in three more days," I pointed out. "They ought to trust you for one night."

"I'm getting awfully nervous about going home, aren't you?"

I nodded. "But Dr. P. keeps saying that's normal. She says we can talk about it in family therapy so it won't be such a big adjustment for everybody."

"My mom's missing family therapy this week, did I tell you?" Lauren said, frowning. "She's going to visit my grandma for the week. She said she needs to get away for a little while."

"Away from what?"

"Me, probably," Lauren said softly.

"That's crazy, Lauren. Talk about negative thinking!"

"Sorry," Lauren said. "I forgot."

For the rest of the afternoon, Lauren still seemed kind of down. Especially after Rachel stopped by to rub it in about how we were missing the Christmas dance. She didn't really *mean* to rub it in, of course. It just always comes out that way with Rachel. What she actually said was that it was too bad about the dance. Then she casually managed to bring up how she already had a date lined up with someone for the spring prom at her preppy school. That's how Rachel is. Even when she's trying to make you feel better, she makes you feel worse. I guess I should give her credit, though. She's improved a lot since I've been here. Lately, I only want to strangle her about every other day.

After dinner that evening, Ms. McG. stopped by and suggested that Lauren and I visit Spencer.

"He hasn't been feeling too hot the past couple days," she said. "I think he'd love a checkers tournament, unless you girls have something else planned for the evening."

"We lead a very active social life," I replied. "But I think we can fit him in. You have to play, though, Lauren. You're the one with the cash. You can afford to lose."

And she did lose, too—three games in a row. After the last one, I shook my head. "Spencer, I know in my heart you're cheating."

"Who, me?" he asked, all angelic innocence.

"But I've been watching your every move, and I can't figure out how you're doing it."

"Hurry up and figure it out, or I'll be broke at this rate!" Lauren said with a laugh.

"I don't cheat. I'm just a lucky guy," Spencer protested.

Not so lucky, actually. He'd been having a rough time with the chemotherapy lately. Twice while we were there, he had to pause to let a bad wave of nausea pass. Ms. McG. had told me that he'd been throwing up all night. I felt so helpless, watching him curl up in pain. Once again, I thought about how often I'd forced myself to throw up, but I tried not to dwell on the guilt.

Even though he felt lousy, I think Spencer liked having us around. When he begged for one last game, Ms. McG. even agreed to let him stay up past his bedtime. He was just about to execute a triple jump over Lauren's last remaining checkers when Sarge appeared in the doorway.

"What on earth are you two doing in here at this hour?" she demanded, hands on her hips.

"Ms. McG. said it would be okay if we played one last—"

"I want you both back in your room, pronto!"

"But—" I started to protest.

"Don't give me any of your lip, Lloyd." She jerked her thumb toward the hallway. "Get a move on!"

"Sorry, Spence," I said.

He quickly jumped his king over Lauren's remaining checkers. "That's a buck you owe me, Lauren," he said triumphantly.

"She can pay you tomorrow, Spencer," Sarge said irritably. "Come on, girls. Get your rears in gear."

"Now I see why they call you Sarge," I muttered as Lauren and I hurried out the door. "It's because of your sunny disposition, isn't it?"

Sarge took a good-natured swat at me as I dashed into our room.

But that wasn't all I dashed into.

I also dashed smack dab into the arms of Daniel Byrne.

"Fancy meeting you here," he remarked.

I untangled myself and gazed around my room in amazement. At least, I *thought* it was my room.

The lights were off, and there were candles burning on my dresser. Red and green crepe paper hung from the ceiling, and silver helium balloons were tied to our beds. Someone had put a portable stereo on Lauren's nightstand. Soft, danceable music was playing. Even more amazing was the fact that Daniel was dressed in a suit, with a pink rose in his lapel. And so was Justin.

Lauren followed me in and gasped. I turned around and realized that the entire staff of Hopeless was standing there in the hallway, watching us with big, goofy grins on their faces. Sarge's was by far the biggest and goofiest.

I gaped at Lauren. Lauren gaped back. In an amazing coincidence, we had both forgotten how to speak at the very same instant.

Fortunately, Justin still remembered how. "Since you couldn't come to the dance," he said softly, "we thought we'd bring the dance to you."

I opened my mouth to speak, but somebody had glued my tongue to the roof of my mouth.

"Well, somebody *say* something," Spencer urged. Ms. McG. had wheeled him down to see the festivities. "By the way, Lauren, you still owe me a buck."

She spun around. "Were all of you in on this?" she demanded.

Ms. McG. nodded. "Justin and Daniel called Dr. Patterson this afternoon," she explained. "Spencer offered to keep you guys occupied while we got things ready. Rachel and Kendra did most of the decorating."

"Not a bad job, either, if I do say so myself," Rachel said.

"It's beautiful," I agreed, having finally discovered my voice.

"Let's give these folks some peace and quiet," Sarge said as she herded everyone down the hall. She even closed our door—something they never let the EDs do.

Suddenly, in the silence that followed, I realized that Lauren and I were standing there next to two guys dressed for a formal dance. She was wearing her gray sweatsuit, and I was attractively dressed in flannel pajamas and my big furry pink slippers with rabbit ears. No makeup. Our hair a mess. It was absolutely humiliating.

"I feel, uh, a little underdressed," I said awkwardly.

"Are you kidding?" Daniel asked with a smile. "Your corsage is going to match those slippers perfectly."

"Corsage?"

He reached for a clear plastic box on my bed and handed it to me. Inside was this beautiful pink rosebud surrounded by baby's breath and pink ribbons. "You put it on your wrist," Daniel said. "Or so my mom tells me."

"I got you yellow," Justin said to Lauren. "Because I know it's your favorite color." He handed her a clear box just like mine.

"I didn't know what your favorite color was," Daniel said apologetically as I slipped the elastic wristband on the corsage over my hand.

I smiled and met his eyes. "Green," I replied. "The color of lime Jell-O."

"Ms. Brady fixed us some special food," Justin said. "They're going to bring it up in a little while. She even made punch."

"This is amazing, Justin," Lauren said. I could tell from the sound of her voice she was a little overwhelmed, but then, so was I.

Daniel took a step closer to me and I realized for the first time that I was easily three or four inches taller than he was. "So, now what?" I asked, trying to sound casual.

Justin glanced over at the stereo. "Well, technically, this is a dance," he said, grinning. "So I guess we should crank up the music." He turned up the stereo, then walked over to Lauren. I watched as he moved closer and took her hand.

Lauren looked over at me. I could tell she was afraid, but she was smiling a little, too. She put her hands on Justin's shoulders and together they began to sway to the music.

Daniel cleared his throat. "So, um, may I have this dance?"

My heart was beating so hard I was sure he could hear it. "I think I should warn you I've never danced before," I said.

He laughed. "I think I should warn you I've never danced before with anyone wearing rabbit slippers."

He reached for my hand, and that's all I remember. The rest of the evening is a wonderful happy blur. Thinking about it now, even a few hours later, I'm starting to wonder if I dreamed the whole thing.

Fortunately, I have evidence. Lauren took a picture of us with the instant camera Justin had brought along. Every time I look at the picture I break out in a smile. It's a little fuzzy, and the lighting's bad, but it's definitely me in my flannel P.J.s and fuzzy slippers, towering over Justin as he stands on his toes to kiss me.

# December 23

Today's the day. Lauren and I are already packed, and now we're just sitting around waiting for our parents to pick us up. We're finally going home. I should be excited. After all, I hate it here at Hopeless. But the truth is, I'm scared to death.

*Home.* Am I really ready to face the real world yet? So much has happened, and so quickly. Dr. P. says that's a natural reaction. She says we have to start taking what we've learned here and making it work in our lives. And of course, we'll still be having therapy sessions with her. "I'm as close as your phone," she keeps telling us. I can call her day or night if I feel like I'm losing control and about to binge. Or if I just need a friend to talk to.

Amazing. I came into this place totally alone, and I'm leaving with two wonderful friends—Dr. P. and Lauren. More than that, really. Everybody here's become a friend, although I hate to admit it. I have to keep up appearances, after all. I have my reputation as a loudmouth complainer to uphold.

Lauren's nervous, too. I can tell. She keeps pacing the room. I finally had to tell her to stop. She was making me seasick.

I know we can do it. At least, I think we can.

Here come Mom and Dad. Time for the real world. Wish us luck.

# December 24

I've been home two days now, and so far, so good. I haven't had a moment to write because I've been so busy. My mom and dad and Cheryl and Brad seem to have every minute planned. This morning it was ice skating. This afternoon, we went shopping. Tonight, caroling. It's been like that ever since I got home from Hopeless. I think Dr. P. told my parents it was important to take my mind off food.

Actually I've been thinking about food a lot, but every time I consider raiding the pantry in the middle of the night, I remember what I learned about riding through my cravings. It's like a wave. It gets bigger and bigger and then it subsides. I just have to breathe deeply and concentrate on being strong. But it's tough, it's really tough.

Daniel's called me two more times. The last time we talked for almost an hour. Mostly we laughed a lot. Have I mentioned what a great laugh he has? But he told me a lot of personal things too. Like how he had been afraid to ask me to the Christmas dance because I was taller than him. I couldn't believe it. It never really occurred to me that guys could be as insecure as girls. I'm so glad he made the basketball team. Even if he doesn't get to play much, I think it'll do wonders for his self-confidence.

I talk to Lauren about fourteen times a day, and we've been over to each other's houses a few times. I'm a little worried about her. She said her parents are arguing a lot, always behind closed doors when they think she can't hear them. I think it's got her scared. And she admitted to me that yesterday she put most of her dinner in her napkin and tossed it out when her parents weren't looking. I made her promise to call me or Dr. P. if she felt like trying a stunt like that again. We have a contract with each other, I reminded her, and I think that made her feel better. I hope so, anyway.

# December 26

I'm really worried. Lauren called me this morning. I expected her to tell me all the great things she got for Christmas. Instead, she told me about something her parents were getting: a divorce.

"Are you sure?" I asked. Lauren can be awfully emotional when it comes to her parents. I figured maybe she'd overheard them arguing and jumped to the wrong conclusion.

"Positive," she replied. Her voice had this eerie, flat tone. "I heard them say it, so I went to my mom and asked her directly. She broke down in tears and admitted it, Zibby. She said they'd been wanting to for a long time." She took a shuddery breath. "It's because of me, you know."

"Of course it's not because of you! Don't be crazy, Lauren."

"I'm not being crazy. Just logical."

"Look," I said. "I'm coming over there right now so we can talk."

"No. I really don't feel like company."

"Then you come over here."

"Later. Tomorrow maybe."

Even over the phone line, I could feel her pulling away from me. "Lauren, I think you should call Dr. P."

"We've got a session on Monday, Zib. I can talk to her then. I'll be fine over the weekend, really."

We went back and forth like that for a while. I could see I wasn't getting anywhere, so when we hung up, I called Dr. P. myself and told her what was going on. She promised to call Lauren and try to arrange an earlier session, just to make sure she was okay.

"What else can I do?" I asked.

"Just what you are doing, Zibby," Dr. P. answered. "Be a good friend."

I'm trying, really I am. But what if that's not enough?

# March 3

It's been over two months since I've written in here. Two months that might as well have been two years. I'm not even sure I remember how to put my feelings on paper.

But I went to Lauren's grave today. And I was filled up with all these things I wanted to say to her, and no place to say them. So I guess I'll say them here. Maybe she's listening. You never know.

I wanted to say I'm not angry with you for dying anymore, Lauren. Oh, I was at first. I hated you all over again for breaking our contract. You knew what you were doing to your body when you stopped eating again. You knew what running miles and miles like that would do to your heart.

But after a while, I started to realize that you didn't think you could handle the pain. After all, nobody understands that pain better than I do. And that made it easier for me to forgive you for giving up. I think you were afraid of all the hard work that went with getting better.

And let me tell you, getting better is not a piece

of cake. (See? I'm still thinking about food even now.) I've had some incredibly rough times, Lauren. I went on two major binges after you died. I think maybe I wanted to die, too. Without you here to help me, I just didn't think I could do it.

Dr. P. put me back in Hopeless after my second binge. I was pretty messed up, as you can imagine. I was lying there, back in our old room, wishing I could just curl up and die, when along comes Spencer with his checkerboard. Only he wasn't in his wheelchair, Lauren. He was walking. He'd finally gotten his new leg. He was still a little wobbly, but that kid can really move, let me tell you. He may give Carl Lewis a run for his money yet.

Spencer did a jog up and down the hall to show off his new leg. At last he had what he'd wanted so badly—the chance to live so he could run. And suddenly I thought of you, Lauren, running and running until you died. Killing yourself with it.

I looked at Spencer and I knew I had a choice. I could be tough, like him, or I could give in to it, like you. And after some thinking, I knew the answer. I'm sorry, Lauren, but I don't want to be like you.

Sure, I still have plenty of bad days. But group gives me a lot of strength. And I see Dr. P. twice a week, too. When I'm really feeling bad, I call Dr. P. or Rachel or Kendra because they'll always understand. (Yes, I know Rachel's a pain.

But I finally figured out that maybe she's such a pain because she's as scared as the rest of us.)

On my very worst days, the days when all I can think about is bingeing, I dig down into my dresser drawer and pull out the picture you took the day of our Great Escape. Remember the one at the park, where I'm sitting there stuffing a donut into my mouth? I look horrible, but that's okay. It reminds me of how far I've come, and how strong I've learned to be.

I've learned some other things, too. Take guys, for instance. Here's the scoop on them. They're not so scary. They're pretty much like us. They just burp louder.

You know what? Daniel knew all along about my bulimia. Right from the very start. Cheryl told him. And you know what else? I've gained a few pounds since we were at Hopeless, and Daniel likes me just the way I am. Will wonders never cease? I guess if you wait long enough, you'll find a guy who likes you for who you are.

But I figured something else out, too. Having a boyfriend doesn't make me happy. *I* make me happy. Daniel's just the frosting on the cake. (I know—more food.)

I guess that's pretty much all I wanted you to say, Lauren. Except to repeat that I really don't hate you anymore for dying. I'm sad that you died, because I know you could have gotten better. And we could have had a lot of laughs together. But I don't hate you.

The truth is, I never really hated you, not even in sixth grade when you ratted on me over the fly incident. The person I hated was me.

But you know what? I don't hate me anymore. Some days I like me more than other days. But I'm really okay, if you give me a chance. And I'm getting better every day.

When it comes right down to it, that's the most important thing I learned at Hopeless House, Lauren.

Hope.

For more information on anorexia and bulimia, contact one of the following organizations:

—Bulimia Anorexia Self-Help, 6150 Oakland Avenue, Deacons Hospital, St. Louis, MO 63139. A twenty-four-hour hot line is available for crisis intervention. Call (314) 768-3292.

—National Association of Anorexia Nervosa and Associated Disorders, P.O. Box 7, Highland Park, IL 60035. A hot line is available between the hours of 9 A.M. and 5 P.M., central time, Monday–Friday. Call (708) 831-3438.

—Anorexia Nervosa and Related Eating Disorders, Inc., P.O. Box 5112, Eugene, OR 97405. For information or referrals, call (503) 344-1144 between 9 A.M. and noon, Pacific time.

—American Anorexia/Bulimia Association, Inc., 418 East 76th Street, NY 10021. Call (212) 734-1114 for information or referrals.

# Look for Beverly Hills, 90210 — the ONLY authorized novels around!

Spelling Ent. Inc.

**Beverly Hills, 90210**
**Beverly Hills, 90210:**
**Exposed!**
**Beverly Hills, 90210:**
**No Secrets**
**Beverly Hills, 90210:**
**Which Way to the Beach**
**Beverly Hills, 90210:**
**Fantasies**
**Beverly Hills, 90210:**
**'Tis the Season**

## Available at bookstores now!

HarperPaperbacks
*A Division of* HarperCollins*Publishers*

bh 1